PORTRAIT OF ELIZA

Ilsa Mayr

For Michael Yuma, a struggling young painter, an upcoming one-man show of his work is the single most important event in his life. This is what he has worked for, hoped for, and dreamed of, and nothing and no one can distract him from it—not even the young woman who so fortuitously stumbled into his world.

An unsuccessful painter herself, heiress Eliza Marshall discovers that the next best thing to being an artist is to be the artist's model, his muse, his strongest supporter, and his object of affection. To assume this role, however, involves lies of omission and deception which she rationalizes by convincing herself that nothing is more important than the paintings. When love is thrown into the mix, Eliza's carefully constructed world of half-truths collapses, threatening all she holds dear.

Only time will tell whether her love of art, and her love for Michael, will be enough to overcome what was said and done.

Other books by Ilsa Mayr:

Dance of Life
Gift of Fortune
A Timely Alibi

PORTRAIT OF ELIZA

•

Ilsa Mayr

AVALON BOOKS
NEW YORK

Published by Thomas Bouregy & Co., Inc.
160 Madison Avenue, New York, NY 10016

Library of Congress Cataloging-in-Publication Data

Mayr, Ilsa.
Portrait of Eliza / Ilsa Mayr.
p. cm.
Novel.
ISBN 0-8034-9763-6 (alk. paper)
I. Title.

PS3613.A97P67 2006
813'.6—dc22
2005035227

PRINTED IN THE UNITED STATES OF AMERICA
ON ACID-FREE PAPER
BY HADDON CRAFTSMEN, BLOOMSBURG, PENNSYLVANIA

This book is dedicated to my critique group,
the wonderful women of Chapter 89.

Chapter One

Eliza Marshall felt the first hollow, growling, gnawing hunger pang—and she hadn't even begun the miserable diet!

Glancing into the big paper cup in her hand, she noted with dismay that there were only a couple sips of chocolate almond latte left. She would have to savor them and make them last, for the austere spa in which she had enrolled would definitely not be serving anything this sinfully delicious.

Before she took another taste, she slowly inhaled the mouthwatering fragrance of coffee—chocolate and almond—wondering again why she had let Rick talk her into spending four weeks of glorious summer on a "fat farm." Was her derriere really that big? Eliza rose from the steps in front of the Chicago Art Institute to look at her reflection in the glass door. Her fashionable patched jeans *were* a little tight. Still, her hips weren't *that* large—at least she did not think so. But Rick obviously did.

He always held up pictures of those anorexic models and television actresses as the ideal of female beauty. She fell far short of that ideal, and could not help but wonder why he bothered with her? It was not as if they were engaged, though they had been dating on and off since her sophomore year in college. Her mother assumed they would marry, of course, but Rick had never actually asked, though he had hinted at marriage, especially recently.

Should she be at least a little bit disappointed that he had not proposed? Uneasily she admitted she might secretly be relieved that he had not. A niggling thought had recurred over the years, and more often in the six months since she had returned from two years of postgraduate study in Paris—something was not quite right about their relationship.

Perhaps it was part of the general discontent and restlessness Eliza felt. She was ready for a change in her life, ready to do something different—but what exactly? She sighed, finished her latte, and entered the Art Institute.

Later, she could not have said how long she stood entranced in front of the Chagall windows before the alarming sense of being watched came over her. The need for vigilance had been deeply drummed into her after the botched kidnapping attempt. At least the police had assumed that the men trying to force Eliza into their van outside her cousin's house had meant to abduct her.

Her loud screams and spirited resistance had saved her by bringing members of the household running.

The subsequent months of life with a bodyguard shadowing her every move had honed her powers of observation. Casually, she glanced around. In the crowded room she saw no one who seemed to take an open interest in her. Yet the feeling persisted as she moved along the courtyard corridor, pausing to admire the ancient statuary and artifacts.

It was still with her three hours later when, saturated with stunningly beautiful visual images, she headed toward the museum coffee shop. To see if she might spot a potential stalker, she decided to stop for a drink and study the people around her. With the fat farm in the back of her mind, Eliza ordered only a bottle of water. She might as well get used to deprivation.

Glancing around, she saw no one who seemed to be following her, but in the crowd moving along the cafeteria-style counters to pick up refreshments, it was hard to tell. She secured one of the tiny tables for two, but no sooner had she sat down than a husky male voice asked her if the other chair were free.

"Yes," she said, glancing at the man.

"Thank you."

Eliza took a second look at him. "You were just looking at the Chagall windows, weren't you?"

"Yeah, me and a few dozen other people," he smiled.

He had not seemed to be watching her in the museum, but every time she had scanned the crowd, she had noticed him. He had looked at the paintings with single-minded intensity and she had found his face fascinating—not exactly handsome, but definitely not easily overlooked. The sharp cheekbones, the slightly hooked nose, the almond-shaped, dark eyes, and the thick, blue-black hair tied back with a leather thong, all hinted at an interesting ethnic mix. *Mediterranean? Native American?*

If she were a gifted rather than barely mediocre portrait artist, she would kill for the chance to paint him—perhaps as a Spanish grandee with dreams of conquests and fierce eyes set on distant horizons, or as a warrior astride a horse every bit as powerful and vital.

"Since you shared your table with me, may I share my cookies with you?" he asked.

A quick glance told her that they were among her favorites—chewy walnut-chocolate-chip-oatmeal. "No, thank you," she said, feeling virtuous. She studied him a moment longer before she blurted, "This may sound crazy but, are you following me?"

"I am."

The unexpectedly frank answer caused her arm to jerk, spilling some water. Anxiety gripped her. Her hand automatically dipped into her shoulder bag and located her cell phone. Having practiced this maneuver, she could dial the number without looking at the phone. She could also feel her panic button in the bag. If she pressed it, help would arrive speedily. However, when she remembered that she was surrounded by dozens of people, her panic subsided.

"I'm sorry," he said, "I didn't mean to startle you." He used a paper napkin to mop up the water she had spilled before he took a card from his pocket and handed it to her.

She read aloud, "Michael Yuma and John Otterman, Sun Designs."

"I'm Michael Yuma."

"What do you design?"

"I don't. I'm the photographer. John is the designer—of women's clothes—clothes that will be available in catalogues and on a web site. If traditional sizes don't fit, women can enter their measurements and our clothes will be adjusted to fit. It's sort of like having your own tailor."

"That's a great idea, but it doesn't explain why you are following me."

"I want you to be one of our models."

Eliza flinched as if he had slapped her. She clutched the table's edge for support and control.

"Are you okay?" Michael said. "What's wrong?"

"How dare you make fun of me? What did I do to deserve being mocked? Did Rick hire you to do this?" she fumed.

"What? I don't know any Rick, and why would you think I am making fun of you? This is a legitimate offer of work. How's that making fun of you?" he asked, sounding somewhat bewildered.

Eliza pressed her eyes shut and prayed to keep the hot tears behind her eyelids.

"Please, answer me. How am I making fun of you?"

"You admitted following me. Are you blind? How could you not have noticed that I wear double-digit-sized jeans? I'm about as suited to be a model as a wild boar is to dancing the *pas de deux* in *Swan Lake*." She grabbed her bag and started to get up, but Michael gently laid his hand on her arm to stop her.

"You didn't give me a chance to explain. It's exactly because you look like a woman ought to look that I want to use you as a model. We don't want to photograph women who look like victims of a refugee camp. John's designing clothes for real women. That's what will make our line of clothing different."

Eliza looked at his hand on her arm. It was strong and well-shaped.

"I also picked you because you have great skin, good bones, a sexy mouth, rich, golden-brown hair, and beautiful, blue-gray, expressive eyes. The camera will love you."

Hearing herself described like that made her flush. It also deprived her of her voice for several stunned seconds. No one had ever told her she looked like that. She had always supposed that most people did not look past her body which, even at its slimmest, did not conform to the sleek lines of a model. She had—as her reed-thin mother had pointed out for as long as Eliza could remember—inherited the full-bodied, curvaceous peasant build and freckles of her war-bride grandmother, Hendrika. But this man liked her skin, freckles and all. Eliza sat back down.

"I know this sounds like a sleazy pickup line, but it isn't. Why don't you come to our studio tomorrow morning at 11:00 and look at our setup? No obligation. If you don't like what you see, you can just walk away. What do you have to lose?"

His voice sounded convincing. She looked into eyes framed by long, thick lashes. She detected nothing other than sincerity and a warm sparkle—but he could be a consummate liar. Still . . .

"Couldn't you use a part-time job?"

"I have a job," she said, exaggerating a little. The job was a volunteer position at the moment, but Eliza was sure she could get something permanent with the agency any time she asked.

"Couldn't you use some extra money? Everyone does."

Not Eliza. She probably had more money than she could spend in a lifetime, thanks to an indecently large trust fund and a thick stock portfolio. If that were not enough, she had a knack for investing wisely, and on top of that, she had a frugal nature. But the offer was intriguing nonetheless—if it was legitimate.

"We can't pay you a lot—not the way the big agencies do—but how about twenty-five dollars an hour? Not bad wages for wearing clothes and holding a pose. Come tomorrow. You don't work on Sundays, do you?"

"We have flex time at work."

"Perfect." He smiled. Then he looked at her thoughtfully, musingly. "I don't normally believe in destiny, but our meeting strikes me as somehow fated. When I went to the Art Institute this afternoon, finding a model was the last thing on my mind. And then I saw you standing in front of the Chagall windows."

"Isn't there more to modeling than wearing clothes? What makes you think I can do it?"

"The way you looked at the displays. With intelligence, total concentration and . . . something like real joy and passion."

Eliza did not know what to say. Michael Yuma was either the most interesting man—or the biggest con artist—she had met in a long time, perhaps ever.

"What's your name?" he asked.

"Eliza Marshall." He extended his hand. Eliza shook it. His shake was firm, the skin on his hands calloused. She hadn't realized that photography was such rough work.

"Well, Eliza, I know you don't quite trust me—"

"It's not that. I—"

"I don't blame you for being cautious, but the offer is legitimate. Come tomorrow and see for yourself. We won't be alone, if that's what's worrying you. John and his wife, Winona, and two other models will be there. Ask someone to come with you, if that'll make you feel more comfortable."

"If I come—and I'm not promising that I will—what do I need to bring?" she asked.

"Nothing. We have everything. Winona's a hairdresser and good with makeup. I hope you'll come." He stood. "If you don't have a car, our place is only half a block from the bus stop. What do you have to lose, a couple of hours of your time? And who knows, this could be the beginning of a new career." Michael smiled at her, picked up one of the cookies and left.

He had a smile that made her feel warm all over. Looking into his eyes was like . . . she struggled to find the right comparison . . . like diving into a pond at midnight, not knowing how deep the water was going to be, how warm or how cold, or how dangerous. She watched him walk away with long, determined strides, like a man who knew exactly where he was going and what he wanted. She envied him that certainty—and the way *his* jeans fit, not too tightly but temptingly molded over strong, well-muscled thighs.

She remained seated, pondering Michael's amazing offer. What *did* she have to lose besides a day on the fat farm? She had already told everyone at Charities, Inc., where she volunteered, that she would be away for the next four weeks. If Michael turned out to be a fraud, she would be only a day late at the spa. If he was legitimate, this could be the beginning of a new chapter in her life—possibly just the change she needed. Since Rick was out of town on a business trip, there was no chance of running into him and being subjected to a lecture.

A kind of excitement she had not felt in a very long time prickled through her blood. She reached for the cookie Michael had left her and bit into it. Delicious. What she needed to complement it was a chocolate almond latte.

"Gran, may I use the pickup today?" Eliza asked at breakfast the next day.

"What on earth for? Is something wrong with your car?" Hendrika Marshall lowered her coffee cup and studied her granddaughter's face.

"No, my car's fine, but I have some errands to run and the pickup would come in handy." Since Michael obviously thought she was not well off, she could hardly arrive in the white Corvette her father had bought her for college graduation—not if she wanted Michael to continue to think she needed the income the modeling job would provide.

As soon as the butler entered to clear the table, Hendrika asked, "Sturges, can we spare the pickup today?"

"Yes, Mrs. Marshall. It's the gardener's day off, and I hadn't planned to drive it."

Eliza smiled, "Thanks."

"You're welcome, Miss Eliza. May I help you in any way?"

"No, thank you, Sturges."

"What are you up to?" Hendrika asked after the butler had left.

"What makes you think I'm up to something?"

"You're vibrating with energy and excitement. I haven't seen you like this since your return from France. I'm not saying that I don't like it. I do. But I am curious about the source of this animation."

"I may be starting a new part-time job."

"Oh? I thought you were checking into that diet clinic today."

"If this job works out, I'll skip the fat farm." Eliza paused a moment. "You know what? Even if it doesn't, I believe I'll cancel my reservation."

"Bravo!" Hendrika applauded heartily. "Frankly, you don't need to go to a fat farm. It's enough that your mother spends her life living on the edge of starvation when she needn't. It's almost sacrilegious. If Gloria had ever been really hungry the way we were during the war in the Netherlands she wouldn't do this to herself. She'd be grateful for the food she had and share what she didn't need with those who go to bed hungry every night." Hendrika paused to take a breath.

Eliza did not say anything. There was nothing she could say. Her mother was obsessed with being thin, but she *was* her mother, and Eliza could not openly side with her grandmother against Gloria. The two women did not get along as it was. Eliza could not remember if the enmity had started before or after her mother divorced Hendrika's son. She also felt a little guilty because, though she loved her mother, she loved *and* liked her grandmother.

"Can you tell me anything about this possible new job?" Hendrika probed gently.

"I'd rather wait until I know if I get it or not."

Hendrika nodded, "Good idea, and I'll hold both thumbs for good luck."

Eliza smiled at the idiom her grandmother had trans- lated literally. "Thanks, Gran. You can also cross your fingers. I can use all the good luck I can get."

"Remember to sign the security log before you leave." Hendrika lifted her hand to forestall Eliza's objection. "I know it's a nuisance listing your destina- tion every time you leave the house, but it makes me feel better. And I'd feel even better if you'd consider accepting a bodyguard again."

"No!" Taking a breath, Eliza said more gently, "I hate being shadowed." She gave her grandmother a sidelong glance. "I have my panic button and my cell phone with the emergency number. Has something happened to make you think I *need* a bodyguard?"

For luck, Hendrika knocked on the highly-polished cherry wood of the dining table. "No, but every day I read about the crazy people out there. I can't help worrying."

"I know. But please try not to worry. I'm always careful. And I'm no longer an eight-year-old who can be grabbed off the street. I'm twenty-five and in good shape." Eliza stood. "Besides, do I look like I'm rich and worth kidnapping?"

Hendrika looked at her granddaughter's patched jeans, faded T-shirt, and scuffed sneakers. "No, you don't," she admitted.

"And I'll be driving a pickup that is dented and hardly new. I'll be careful." Eliza kissed her grandmother's cheek, wrote down the address in the security log at the door, and headed for the garage.

Hendrika watched her granddaughter back out of the garage before she rang for Sturges.

He appeared almost instantly. He read Eliza's entry before he approached his employer.

"Please see what you can find out about my granddaughter's possible employers."

"Sun Designs," Sturges said, adding the address from memory. "I'll get right on it." Sturges exchanged a look of perfect understanding with his employer and left.

Having studied the city map the night before, Eliza had no trouble locating Sun Design Studio in the Rogers Park area. She drove past the studio twice, studying the neighborhood before she parked the truck. The ingrained habit of checking her surroundings made her watch the street for several minutes before she got out of the truck.

When she entered the office, Michael looked up from the camera he was loading and walked toward her with a smile. In the few seconds it took for him to reach her, she noticed that his smile lit up his dark eyes, that his jeans were clean and ironed, that the white, tucked-in shirt looked even whiter against the bronzed skin of his face, neck, and forearms. Just looking at him made her throat tighten and her pulse beat faster.

"I can't tell you how glad I am that you came," he said.

"Don't be too glad until you take some photos and see if I'm suitable." Her voice was low and soft and lacked the warning her words had intended to carry.

"I'm not worried about that. Let me show you around and introduce you to everyone."

Everyone included John and his very pregnant wife, Winona, who were adding accessories to the outfits laid out on three long tables, and two models—a lovely, dark-eyed brunette and a statuesque, green-eyed blonde. Eliza was relieved to see that neither girl was noticeably thinner than she was.

"This used to be a restaurant," Michael explained. "We converted the dining room into offices and the kitchen into a dark room for me, a dressing room for the models, and a lounge area for all of us. It's got a fridge and microwave if you want to bring your lunch tomorrow."

It amazed her that he really did not seem to have any doubts that she would be photogenic. She was far from feeling that confident herself. What made her even more anxious was that she realized she very much wanted to come to Sun Designs every day—to model, of course, *and* to see him, she admitted to herself. Then she sighed. Unless her luck with relationships suddenly changed, she was probably doomed to disappointment.

"Don't look so worried. You'll do just great. I have a good eye for shape, color, and line and a good deal of experience."

Just what did that mean? Experience in what and with whom?

"Let's go into the studio and shoot a few pictures," he said, leading the way.

"What do you want me to do?"

"Sit in that chair." Michael adjusted some lights. "Turn a little sideways. Lift your chin just a bit."

She could not see him because of the bright light he had turned on her, but she heard the camera click in rapid succession.

"Talk to me, Eliza."

"What shall I talk about?"

"Anything. I want you to relax. You're a little tense. Um . . . tell me about your first apartment. Where was it?"

"In Paris. In the attic of an old three-story building on the Left Bank." Actually, it was her first and only apartment as she had lived mostly in boarding schools and college dormitories and with her grandmother between semesters.

"Sounds like the proverbial starving-artist's garret," he said.

*It had been only a would-be artist's garret, unfortu-
nately, but she had not been starving.* "My neighbor
was a painter. He was quite good."

"Oh, yeah? Could he make a living at it?" Michael
asked.

"No, he worked as a waiter in a cafe at night. He'd
come home after midnight and then was up by seven to
paint. He liked the morning light."

"Sounds like you admired him."

"I did. He had talent and worked very hard. He knew
what he wanted."

"Were you in love with him?"

She smiled and shook her head. "No. He had a girlfriend."

"And she modeled for him."

"How did you guess that?" Eliza asked.

"That's every painter's dream."

"And every photographer's?"

"Could be."

Eliza hoped he would expand on that, but he did not.
Bummer. How could she ask him if he had a girlfriend
without being rude or shamelessly revealing her interest in him? Come to think of it, she did not know if he
had a wife, though something about him gave her the
feeling that he did not. That, of course, could have been
pure wishful thinking on her part.

"Turn so I can see that interesting profile of yours. It
could be straight off an ancient Greek sculpture."

She did as he asked, trying to remember what the
noses on ancient Greek sculptures looked like. *Is an
interesting profile good or bad?*

"Relax. I can see tension in your neck. Take two deep breaths."

He waited until she had done so. Then she heard the camera click several times.

"Turn to face me. What did you do in Paris?"

"I studied."

"Lucky you. What did you study?"

"Mostly the language." That was true, but mainly because she had been forced to speak the language daily. It had not been the subject of her formal study.

"Please stand behind the chair. Place one hand on it." Michael adjusted the lights. "Shift your weight to your left foot. Good."

The shutter clicked repeatedly.

"Turn a little to the side. So, in Paris you lived in a garret. Where do you live here in Chicago?"

"Right now I live with my grandmother. It's just until I find an apartment of my own," she added hastily. It was time for her to move out on her own. Why had she not done this before? She would start the hunt for an apartment as soon as she left the studio. That decision made, she felt incredibly good.

"Hold that expression," Michael said. "This is great. Just great."

When he paused for a moment, she asked, "What expression?"

"Kind of happy and surprised. What were you thinking?"

"I just decided to look for an apartment of my own as soon as we're through here."

"Do you have any leads?"

"No," she confessed, and her mood plummeted.

"I noticed a For Rent sign at an apartment complex four blocks north of here. You might want to check that out. The apartments are basically okay except they need a good cleaning and maybe a coat of paint. Most important, the rent's affordable. And the neighborhood's become a lot safer than it used to be."

"Thanks, I'll take a look. Do you live in this area?"

"I have a studio near here with living quarters behind it."

"A photo studio?"

"No." He turned off the bright lights. "We're through here. Winona will help you with your makeup."

Eliza was dying to find out what kind of studio he had, if he lived alone, and if he had a girlfriend, but could not think of a polite way of asking him such personal questions.

When they stopped for lunch Eliza gladly accepted a sandwich from Winona, saving her a trip to the nearest fast food restaurant. She made a mental note to ask Sturges to pack some lunch meat, cheese, and bread to put into the studio's refrigerator.

Promptly at 1:00 Michael resumed taking pictures. Eliza, like the other two models, posed in four outfits for him. They quit at 3:30.

She moved her head from side to side, easing the tension in her neck and shoulders.

"Tired?" Michael asked.

"Yes. I didn't realize modeling was so demanding. I'm beat."

"It'll get easier," he promised.

"Does that mean I have the job?" Eliza asked, hardly daring to breathe.

"Of course. I'm sorry, I thought you understood that when I asked you to wear the outfits."

"I wasn't sure. I needed to hear you say so." Eliza smiled happily. Then growing serious, she asked, "Where was that apartment you mentioned?"

"It's not far. Want me to go with you to show you the way?"

"That would be great. Shall I follow you? I'm parked up the street."

"So am I. Let's go."

They would spend some time together. Eliza's heart leaped with joy. She thought she should hide the happiness she felt, but could not refrain from smiling at him.

And he smiled back.

As they walked from room to room in the apartment, Michael watched her. Eliza moved with an unstudied grace that suggested she might have taken dancing lessons as a young girl. He liked the way she held her body, no jerky movements, no fidgeting. She had perfect posture.

She touched the wall.

"Definitely needs a new coat," he said. When she looked startled, he added, "Of paint. Have you ever painted?"

"Walls? No."

"The carpet isn't too bad. A good shampooing and

it'll look almost like new." Watching her face he added, "I suspect you've never shampooed a rug."

"I haven't."

"Led a spoiled, middle-class life?" he asked, softening his question with a smile.

Eliza shrugged, "Sort of . . . but I'm a quick learner. If you show me how to do something once, I can usually do it."

She had a great attitude. He had noticed that at the shoot. And she *was* a quick learner. He had noticed that, too.

Eliza stopped in front of the bedroom closet. Michael followed her. He was close enough to smell the fragrance she wore. He could not identify it, but it was pleasing to his senses. Subtle, yet seductive, the scent made him think of that particular shade of green he had not been able to mix to his satisfaction—it was the green of new leaves touched with that hint of blue that certain pines took on at dusk. He inhaled, committing the scent to memory.

"The closet's a little small," Eliza murmured.

"You like to shop?"

"I loathe it!" She looked at him over her shoulder. "Now you wonder why a woman who loathes shopping needs a larger closet?"

"Why does she?"

"Because she has a mother who lives to shop, and every time Mom hits the stores, she buys something for her daughter."

"Your tone suggests you don't always like what your mother buys."

"I never like what she buys—well, rarely. She likes that town-and-country, yuppie look, which I find abysmally boring."

"What do you like?" Michael asked, intrigued.

"Peacock colors, rich fabrics from Southeast Asia, batik, tie-dye, and peasant prints."

"I've been known to create some terrific tie-dye T-shirts." Michael placed his hands on her shoulder. "Turn around so I can see if I have one that might fit you."

She did.

Her long, golden-brown hair brushed against his hands. His skin felt as if it had been touched by fine silk. When she placed her hands lightly against his chest, he felt as if a light electric charge sizzled through his flesh.

It had been a mistake to touch her. It reminded him of all he had renounced. He had no time for women. He had no money to spend on them. All his energy, all his resources, had to be focused on his work. Eliza of the sun-kissed hair and dove-gray eyes was off limits. She had to be, for a woman like her—beautiful, spoiled, middle-class—would expect to be wooed, which took time. And she would expect to be wined and dined, which took money. He had neither. It was just his rotten luck to meet a woman like her at this critical juncture in his life.

Quickly he stepped back. He noticed Eliza's startled look but ignored it.

"I'm sure I have a T-shirt that'll fit you. If you've seen enough, let's go back to the landlord's office."

Chapter Two

"Gran, I have already given the landlord a deposit on the apartment. It's a done deal," Eliza said, her tone firm. She saw Hendrika and Sturges exchange a look. "What?" she asked.

"I'm a little concerned. The area is not the safest," Hendrika said.

"How can you say that? I'll bet you've never even been to Rogers Park."

"I haven't, but Sturges has, and I trust his judgment."

"There's no such thing as a safe area," Eliza stated, her voice calm but filled with conviction. "That's what the investigator who worked on the attempted abduction said. Remember? But there are rules for safe behavior. And I learned those well. He made sure of that. I lived by myself in Paris and nothing happened."

"Chicago isn't exactly Paris," Hendrika pointed out.

"True, but I can handle myself. I'm having an alarm system installed. The apartment complex is full of young people. I'll blend right in." With a frown, she added, "Except for one thing."

"And what's that?"

"My car. I can't take the Corvette. I'd have to park it on the street and it would probably be stolen the first night. I need to buy a used car." Eliza saw Sturges step closer, an interested expression on his usually dead-pan face.

"What kind of car do you have in mind?" Hendrika asked.

"Something like your pickup. It's old enough that it wouldn't get stolen, but in good enough shape that it would be reliable. Also, it would be handy to haul stuff to the apartment, which is unfurnished, except for a stove and fridge."

"Sturges, when were we planning to replace our pickup?" Hendrika asked.

"In the spring."

"Is there any reason why we can't do it now?"

"No reason," Sturges said.

"Then go and buy one."

"Yes, ma'am," Sturges said.

He looked as if he wanted to rub his hands in anticipation. His only weakness, Eliza suspected, was his love of cars. He used one stall in the garage to work on old cars in his free time. Except he did not call them old. He called them "classic."

"Then it's settled."

"Gran, you've lost me. What's settled?"

"I'm giving you the pickup, of course."

"I appreciate that, but I can't *take* it. I'll buy it from you, though. Will you sell it to me? Please?"

Hendrika stared at her granddaughter's eager face for several seconds before she turned to the butler again. "Sturges, how much is the truck worth?"

"We just put in a new battery, so I think seven thousand dollars should cover it."

Hendrika nodded. "I'd much rather *give* you the pickup—"

"No, absolutely not. I'm buying it. I have the money. Gran, this is important to me. Okay?" Before her grandmother could change her mind, she said, "It's a deal. This is so exciting. An apartment of my own and now a pickup."

Hendrika smiled at her. She had not seen Eliza this lively and enthusiastic in a long time. She hated to accept money for the truck, but realized that this was another step in Eliza's quest for independence.

"I'll write a check. Then what do I have to do?" Eliza asked.

"Sturges will explain it to you." While the butler did just that, Hendrika studied her granddaughter. Eliza had grown up a lot during her time in France. Hendrika was glad she had urged her son to let his daughter go abroad. She had sorely missed Eliza, but the sacrifice had been worth it.

There was no longer any danger that Eliza would develop into a selfish social butterfly, intent only on her own pleasure. Hendrika felt tremendous relief about that. Now if she could only get Rick out of her darling girl's life and find her an honorable, hard-working young man, she could die a happy woman.

Eliza sat in the middle of the floor of her empty living room, turning the pages of a book. A knock on the open door made her look up.

"Michael, come on in," she said with a smile.

"You shouldn't leave your door open. It's not safe."

"I usually don't. I left it open for Sturges who's bringing a stepladder." She uncurled herself and rose in one smooth move.

Who is Sturges? Her boyfriend? The idea did not appeal at all to Michael but what had he expected? Eliza was a beautiful young woman. She probably had several men chasing after her. Just because he had not made a pass at her in the week he had been working with her, did not mean other men had or would not. And that was as it should be.

He certainly could not go out with her. He had not budgeted any money or time for dating in the plan he had set up last New Year's Day. This was his breakout year. Nothing could interfere with that—not even the very lovely, very sexy, very desirable Eliza who made his palms sweat and blood course through his veins.

"What are you reading?" he asked to break the silence.

"A book on how to clean everything."

"You're kidding, right?"

"No." She closed the book so that he could see the title. "Don't laugh," she said. "It's been very helpful. For example, when you wash dirty walls you start at the bottom and work your way up. Otherwise you get streaks that show up under a coat of paint. Did you know that?"

Michael shook his head.

"And here I thought you were an experienced paint-er." She clucked her tongue and slanted him a mock disapproving look.

"I am a very experienced painter. But my mother always got the walls ready. I didn't pay any attention to how she did that."

"Are you close to your mother?" The question obviously surprised him. He did not say anything for several seconds. "Did I say something wrong? If so, I'm sorry," Eliza said.

"No, you didn't say anything wrong. I was trying to figure out if this was one of those trick questions women ask—you know, to see if a man is sensitive . . . in touch with his feelings, stuff like that."

"Trick question? How?"

"Well, if I say, yes, I'm close to my mother, you might dismiss me as being a mama's boy. If I say no, you might cast me in the role of an insensitive jerk who doesn't appreciate women. Either way, I'm in trouble." She looked at him with wide, surprised eyes, eyes of the most intriguing shade of blue-gray he had ever seen. In his mind Michael mixed colors on his palette, trying to come up with that shade. If he were to paint her—and his fingers were aching to do so—

"I really didn't think along those lines," Eliza assured him. "You said you helped your mother, so I wondered if you were close. That's all. Honestly."

"In that case, yes, I'm close to my mother."

Michael had said it without even a trace of self-consciousness. Eliza liked that. It had to be great to feel that way. "Does your mother live in Chicago?"

"No. She's in South Dakota."

"Is that your home state?"

"Yes. How about you? Where are you from?"

"Chicago."

"Really? You're the first person I've met here who's actually *from* Chicago. That's probably—" Michael broke off, looking at the man who stood in the open doorway, trying to catch his breath while balancing an armful of bags and a stepladder. "Can I help you?" Michael asked.

"Thanks. I would appreciate it, if you could take the ladder," Sturges said.

"Sure thing." Michael took the ladder while Sturges placed two large bags on the floor.

Eliza rushed forward to open them. "Great, You brought the paint. Thanks," she smiled. "Sturges, this is Michael Yuma, the photographer. You've heard me speak of him."

The men shook hands and murmured the appropriate words.

Michael was pleased to observe that Sturges was old enough to be Eliza's father. Not that the age difference necessarily ruled out a rival. *Rival? How had that word snuck into his brain?*

"Is there anything else I—"

"No, no," Eliza said hastily, not wanting Sturges to address her as "Miss Eliza." "Thanks. I can take it from here."

"Are you a painter?" Michael asked.

"Sturges works for my grandmother," Eliza replied quickly. "And she's expecting you back, isn't she, Sturges?" Eliza touched the butler's arm and glanced meaningfully toward the door.

"Yes she is, so I had better hurry back."

Thank heaven Sturges was good at taking hints. Eliza closed the door after bidding him good-bye.

"What does Sturges do for your grandmother?"

"Whatever needs to be done. Sturges is a man of many talents. He showed me how to paint a room. Want to see the result?" Eliza led the way to the bedroom. "*Voila!*"

"Nice job. Are you painting everything white?"

"Yes. The windows in this old building are not very big. White will make the rooms look lighter and bigger, and it'll go with everything. Don't you agree?"

Michael nodded. He pried the lid off the gallon can and stirred the paint.

"What are you doing?" Eliza asked.

"Getting ready to paint. Are you going to join me or just stand there watching?"

"Michael, I can't let you spend your Saturday evening helping me paint."

"Why not?"

"I'm sure you have something better to do."

"Such as?"

"Well, such as . . . having a date?"

"No date tonight. Do you have one?" Michael asked casually, though he could feel his heart beat faster in anticipation of her reply.

"No."

He liked that answer a lot. "In that case, why don't we get this room painted? If we work at it, we could get it done in a couple of hours."

"Really, you don't have to help," Eliza said.

"I know that, but I want to. We're practically neighbors, and helping you move in is the neighborly thing to do."

"All right, but on one condition. You'll stay for pizza after we're finished."

"Make it thick crust with sausage and green peppers and you've got a deal."

"You're on." Eliza smiled happily. When the symphony on the radio in the kitchen swelled to a crescendo, she said, "I forgot to ask if you like classical music. Shall I change the station?"

"Classical is fine. We use rock during a shoot because the tempo works better for modeling. Something about rock energizes everyone. Or so it seems to me."

Eliza agreed with him.

True to Michael's prediction, they finished painting the room in just a little over two hours. While he washed the brushes and the roller, Eliza ordered the pizza.

"What would you like to drink?" she asked, studying the contents of her refrigerator. "There's pop, diet pop, red wine, and bottled water."

"A pop sounds good," Michael said, giving the brushes and the roller a final rinse. "We work well together, don't we? If this is your first time painting, you are a quick study."

"It's my first time painting walls, but I have spent years trying to learn to paint on canvas."

Michael paused in the act of placing the tools on the paper towels Eliza had spread on the counter. "Are you still painting?"

"No."

"Why not?"

"Because I'm not good enough."

"Are you sure? Maybe you just got discouraged. It's very hard to show or even to get gallery space to hang a single painting."

"I'm dead sure. Believe me, I wish I weren't, but I am. I'm good enough technically to do illustrations or teach art in a school, but that's it. I love and admire good painting too much to continue. The world does not need another third-rate painter."

"Did your teachers agree with your evaluation?"

"Yes."

"I'm sorry," Michael frowned sympathetically.

"Don't be. They merely confirmed the conclusion I had reached on my own. Technique can carry you only so far. I simply wasn't born with that magical some-thing that makes a great painter." She shrugged.

"So you're at a crossroad now. What do you think you want to do with your life?"

Eliza grinned, "What do I want to be when I grow up?" Then growing serious she said, "I took a couple of classes in art and play therapy for kids this spring and I really enjoyed it. And I've been working with teenagers and children. I like that, too. Maybe I can combine the two."

"Isn't working with teens hard?"

"Oh, yes," Eliza said emphatically. "But we click—as much as anyone can click with that age group." She shrugged again. "What about *you*?"

Michael raised a dark eyebrow. "What about me?"

"You said you had a studio and that it wasn't for photography. Are you a sculptor?"

"What makes you think that?"

Eliza reached out and turned his hand palm-side up. She rubbed her thumb over his skin. "These calluses. In Paris I met a couple of sculptors and their hands looked just like yours."

He had thought that calluses were just thick, lifeless skin until Eliza touched them. Suddenly they were as sensitive and receptive as nerve endings. He had to swallow before he could speak. "These I got working construction."

"I don't understand. You're obviously a very good photographer. What were you doing working in construction?"

"Earning money. Construction pays well, especially when you're working on a building that's behind schedule and the boss gives you lots of overtime. John and I needed the money to get our clothing line started." Eliza released his hand. Michael would have enjoyed her holding it a little longer.

"I imagine that took quite a bit of capital," she said.

"Sure did. We pooled our savings but still had to take out a loan."

"I hope you used a reputable bank that isn't gouging you with high interest rates."

She looked genuinely concerned. Michael could not remember any woman expressing an interest in his business, much less being concerned over interest rates. He was curious. "You sound as if you know quite a bit about loans and interest rates."

"Doesn't everybody?" Eliza asked lightly, not adding that she had grown up with conversation about the banking business at every meal. She came from a long line of financiers. Her father was president of one of the few family-owned banks left in the state, and he was grooming her brother to take over the business when he retired.

Thank heaven for Peter. If not for him, her father would have recruited *her* to carry on the family tradition. And knowing her father, who was a master at wheeling, dealing, and instilling guilt, Eliza would inevitably have grit her teeth, donned bankers' gray, and soldiered on in banking and high finance.

The doorbell rang. "Pizza's here. Perfect timing." Eliza grabbed her purse and rushed to the door. She took the large box, paid the delivery boy, tipping him generously, and turned to Michael.

"As you can see," she said, gesturing around the room, "I don't have a table or chairs yet. Sorry, but we'll have to sit on the floor. Will you grab the table-cloth that's in the middle drawer next to the sink?" Sturges had brought it when he had delivered a lunch basket from her grandmother.

Michael spread the cloth on the floor. "I'll get the drinks. What do you want?"

"A diet orange pop, please."

Michael brought it to her. He had chosen a root beer for himself.

"I'm sorry I don't have the real thing." When he looked puzzled, she added, "A real beer. Don't most guys like beer?"

"I don't. I saw too much drinking on the reservation to enjoy it."

The reservation. So, her guess about his ethnic background had been correct. That pleased her. And he was not a drinking man. That pleased her even more.

"I saw a lot of drinking in college," Eliza said. "I didn't like what it did to my friends." She grinned. "Besides, I'd rather spend calories on food than alcohol. Speaking of calories, let's eat."

They sat cross-legged on the floor. Eliza handed Michael a paper napkin. "Help yourself." She waited until he had taken a bite of pizza and saw him nod in approval before she helped herself.

Michael ate neatly and with obvious enjoyment. He did not keep count of how many pieces he ate, unlike Rick who counted every calorie he put into his mouth. The man was obsessed with keeping his thirty-inch waistline.

Michael was lean too, but it was the tough, muscular leanness from hard physical work. A sexy leanness that appealed mightily to Eliza, making her want to touch those broad shoulders and strong arms. She quickly averted her eyes, not wanting him to catch her looking at him with undisguised longing.

"You still haven't told me what kind of studio you have," she said. "Is it a secret?"

Michael grinned at her, "Hardly . . . I'm a painter."

Eliza stopped chewing to stare at him. What were the odds of meeting a man she liked and found attractive who was also involved in something she loved so passionately? Swallowing, she asked, "You're a painter? Really?"

"Really. All the other jobs I've done and am doing are merely the means to earn enough money to let me paint without interruption for the next six months or so."

"Why six months?" Eliza asked, intrigued.

"In six months I should be able to paint enough canvases for a one-man exhibition."

"Wow. You're that good? To have your own show?" she asked stunned, before she realized that he might find her reaction tactless. She felt herself blush. "I'm sorry. I didn't mean—"

"That's okay. The owner of a respectable gallery thinks I'm good enough to have my own exhibition . . . in his place."

"That's terrific! Has he shown any of your paintings?"

"Several . . . even sold a couple."

"Congratulations. Obviously you're good." Eliza lifted her pop can. "Here's to your one-man show."

"Thanks, Eliza."

"What's the name of the gallery?" When he told her, she did not even try to hide how impressed she was. "I know it well. Does he have any of your paintings now?"

"Yes. Three landscapes and a still life."

"I hope he hasn't sold them yet." Seeing Michael's

surprised expression, she added, "I mean, I'd like to see them before he sells them."

He smiled at her. "One of these days I'll give you a tour of my studio and show you the paintings I have there."

"You will? That's wonderful. I'd love to see them." Eliza bit her lip to stop herself from asking him to name the day and the hour.

Ordinarily Michael did not care what people thought of his paintings. He painted to please himself, listening to the voice within that told him how and what to paint. But he suddenly discovered he wanted Eliza to like his work and the realization stunned him. He stared blindly at the slice of pizza in his hand.

"Michael? Is something wrong?"

"Wrong?"

"With the pizza."

"No, no, it's fine." He quickly took a bite. She was perceptive and intelligent. He would have to watch himself with her and remember his resolution not to date for the next six months. Suddenly that seemed like an unendurably long time.

When Eliza returned to her grandmother's house it was after eleven. Surprised to find Hendrika still up, Eliza joined her in the small sitting room her grandmother favored.

Hendrika had been listening to a public radio program while she worked on some intricate embroidery. Seeing Eliza, she turned off the radio.

"I just rang Sturges for some mint tea. Will you join me?"

"No, thanks, Gran. I'm still stuffed. We didn't eat until after we finished painting the living room."

"Who's we?"

"Michael and I. I told you about him, remember?"

"Oh, yes. The photographer for whom you model clothes." Hendrika peered at her granddaughter over the special glasses she wore for close work. "He came to help you paint your living room on a Saturday night?"

"Yes. Isn't that great? I thought Sturges would have told you."

"He mentioned meeting Michael. When can I meet him?"

"When you come to my apartment. But first I have to get some furniture. I can't very well ask you to sit on the floor."

"Thank you, dear, I appreciate that. I'm afraid I'd make an ungraceful spectacle of myself, getting down and up from the floor." Hendrika paused for a moment. Casually she asked, "Why not bring Michael here? For dinner, perhaps . . . or lunch."

"No!" Realizing how overly emphatic she had sounded, Eliza calmly added, "That wouldn't be a good idea."

Sturges entered and set down the tea tray. He poured a cup and handed it to Hendrika.

"Thank you again, Sturges, for bringing the paint and the stepladder," Eliza said. "I also want to thank you for . . . you know, leaving so quickly. I hope I didn't offend you."

"You didn't, Miss Eliza."

"Oh, good." Eliza smiled at him, relieved. "One more thing. Could you please not call me 'Miss Eliza' in front of Michael? Actually, you don't have to call me that here either."

"We've discussed this before, and you know I would feel very uncomfortable not calling you Miss Eliza. However, I'll try not to do so in the young man's presence."

"I'd appreciate that. Thank you, Sturges."

The moment Sturges closed the door behind him, Hendrika asked, "Eliza, what are you up to?"

"Up to? Nothing."

"Eliza, I wasn't born yesterday. Why don't you want to bring Michael to meet me here?" She studied her granddaughter's face. "You haven't told him the truth, have you? Who you are, where you live—"

"I haven't lied to him," Eliza protested quickly.

"Withholding part of the truth is lying by omission," Hendrika pointed out gently. "An old-country expression comes to mind. 'Lies have short legs.' They can't run very fast. The truth catches up before you know it, and bites you in the behind."

"Gran, you don't understand," Eliza cried out desperately. "Michael thinks I'm just a regular person. Sort of poor. Well, maybe not exactly poor, but certainly not really, really rich. You don't know how wonderful it is to be just a woman. He doesn't look at me and see dollar signs."

"My dear, I understand better than you think. Is there a chance that you might get serious about him?" Hendrika watched Eliza's eyes light up.

"Oh, Gran, he's a painter! He's doing all the other work to save money so he can paint enough to mount a one-man show. He must be good, because Kuenstler and Sons offered him the exhibition. They wouldn't do it if he weren't truly talented."

"But is there a chance that you *both* will get serious?"

"I don't know. I certainly like him better than any man I've ever met. I like him a lot, *and* he's a painter. Gran, it doesn't get any better than that!" Eliza paused and sighed biting her lip. Her forehead wrinkled in thought. "I don't know how he feels about me," her expression brightened, "but he helped me find an apartment, and he helped me paint it. That has to mean something." She lifted her shoulders in a shrug.

Then she smiled. "It's too early to speculate about all this. I don't want to analyze it to death. Right now I'm enjoying the modeling and being with him and getting my apartment ready. I'm having a great summer."

"What about Rick?"

Eliza frowned. "What about him? I was never in love with him. And he was never serious about me. He was just sort of part of our crowd," she shrugged.

Hendrika had no illusions about Rick and knew that Eliza was at least wrong partly. Rick was serious about the Marshall family connection—and Eliza's trust fund. He was probably not in love with Eliza but, encouraged by Gloria, he had certain expectations. Hendrika was sure about that.

Eliza took a deep breath. "The only thing I really need is a real, full-time job—one that pays a salary. And I have some ideas about that." She kissed her grandmother's cheek. "I'm going to bed. Painting rooms is hard work. Good night, Gran."

Hendrika watched her granddaughter leave, suspecting she was already half in love with this young painter. But her happiness for Eliza was tempered by the fact that she had not told Michael the truth. Lies, even little white ones, often backfired. Hendrika resolved to say a few extra prayers before she went to sleep.

Chapter Three

On Monday morning Eliza paced back and forth in front of the Kuenstler Gallery. She kept glancing at her watch, hoping they might open a few minutes early. Finally, at one minute after ten, a man unlocked the door.

Eliza dashed past the surprised salesman. She had been sitting on the proverbial pins and needles all weekend, waiting to see Michael's paintings.

"May I help you?" the man asked. His expression indicated that he very much doubted it.

Chagrined, Eliza realized that she was not dressed in a manner suggesting she could afford even the least expensive piece in the gallery. She briefly flirted with the idea of adopting the imperious tone her mother used with people who annoyed her, but since Eliza was not sure she could pull it off, she decided on a friendly approach.

"Will you please point me toward the paintings by young, contemporary American artists?"

"I'm not sure we have any," the man said with an indifferent shrug.

Refusing to be dismissed, Eliza squared her shoulders. "I'm sure you do. I've been to your gallery several times—even to a couple of openings that were by invitation only."

His fair skin reddened. He put on an expression of deep thought.

"Oh, yes," he said, "I seem to recall now that we might have something along those lines. Follow me, please."

Eliza had not wanted to ask specifically for Michael's paintings. Doing that often increased the price. She would not mind if the increase were passed on to the artist, but she strongly suspected that it would not be.

"Here we are," the clerk said, indicating a small room before them.

Eliza's eyes quickly roamed across the nearest wall before she made a beeline for the autumn landscape. The signature in the lower right-hand corner confirmed her guess. How had she known this was Michael's painting? Had she picked it because it was the best of the group? Or had something in the painting held traces of him that had called out to her?

She had no trouble locating his other landscapes. All of them were strong. Each brush stroke had been placed firmly, thoughtfully, without hesitation. Michael knew what he wanted, and it showed in his paintings.

It took her a little longer to spot the still life, but only because it was in a different medium. A small water-color, it featured a simple quart canning jar filled with a handful of wild flowers sitting on a rough, scarred, painted table. An open book with a blade of grass to mark the page lay on the corner. The composition was perfect; the colors delicate, yet strong. Eliza lusted after this painting. She had to have it.

She clasped her hands behind her to keep from grab-bing the still life and finding herself hauled off to the nearest police station. Since she did not want Michael to know that she had bought the painting, she could not use her credit card or write a check. And she did not have enough cash in her wallet.

Could she risk leaving the gallery long enough to sprint to the nearest bank? What were the chances of someone else coming in this early on a Monday morn-ing and buying the still life while she was out getting the cash? On a rational level she knew the chances were slim-to-none, but on an emotional level she was ner-vous.

Taking a deep breath, she said to the clerk, "I'll be back." Eliza did not think he looked convinced. Al-though she managed to keep herself from running out of the gallery, once outside she darted between the win-dow shoppers on Michigan Avenue to reach the bank.

Twenty-three breathless minutes later she faced the surprised clerk once again.

"I want to buy the small still life," she told him.

"Did you notice the price, Miss?"

"Of course I did." She watched his wide-eyed

expression as she pulled out a fistful of large-denomination bills from her purse. Without a word he went to get the painting.

When he returned he asked, "Where shall I send it?"

"Just wrap it up please. I want to take it with me."

He opened his mouth and closed it. "As you wish, Miss."

When he asked for her name and address for the receipt, she gave her grandmother's maiden name. She could not risk Michael finding out she had bought the painting. Even though the cost of the small watercolor had not been exorbitant, it was unlikely that a woman who was going to furnish her apartment with items bought in second-hand stores and flea markets could afford it. It also meant she could not keep the watercolor in her apartment. Eliza sighed. She would have loved to hang it between the windows in her bedroom where she could see it first thing each morning.

On the way to her truck, an idea struck her. She took her cell phone from her purse and dialed her mother's number.

"Hi, Mom. Did I wake you?"

"No. On weekdays I get up to have a cup of coffee with Charles before he leaves for the office. You know that," Gloria said.

Eliza couldn't recall whether she did or not, so she merely made a murmur that could be interpreted as agreement.

"Are you calling from the spa?" Gloria asked.

It took a second before Eliza realized her mother was referring to the fat farm. "No, I'm here in Chicago. I decided not to go." Eliza could feel the disapproval travel through the phone connection even before her mother spoke.

"That's too bad. Does Rick know?"

"No, I haven't talked to him."

"He'll be so disappointed. He won't show it, of course, because he has such lovely manners."

That is just about all he has, Eliza added silently. As for his disapproval—oh, yes, he would show it. She had been the recipient of his subtle but devastating criticism often enough that she could recall it vividly. She shuddered at the thought. Never again would she put herself through that. She was finished with Rick. Actually, she had been finished with him for a long time but had just not formally admitted it. She would have to do that now. She did not look forward to telling him, but since he was out of town for several more weeks, she did not have to worry about his reaction for the time being.

"Don't you care that you let Rick down?" her mother asked in the lengthening silence between them.

Eliza suspected that her mother meant, *Didn't she care that she had let her mother down.* "Frankly, Mom, I'm no longer terribly interested in what Rick thinks." She thought she heard the sound of a sharply indrawn breath, but ignored it.

"I need to speak to my stepfather. Is he there?"

"Eliza, you're not seriously thinking of taking Charles up on his offer to work for his brokerage firm? I'm sure he only made the suggestion because you were so undecided about what you wanted to do."

"Mother, are you saying I'm not smart enough to become a stockbroker?"

"Of course not. You seem to have inherited the Marshall gene for handling anything to do with money. But, Eliza, please! Being a stockbroker is such an unfeminine profession."

Eliza could picture the expression of distaste on her mother's delicately-featured, beautiful face. She looked up at the blue patch of sky between the tall buildings and repressed a sigh of exasperation.

"I only want to ask Charles about a stock I'm interested in," she improvised. "Is he still at home?"

"No. He left for his office an hour ago."

"Thanks. I'll call him at work." Eliza broke off the conversation before it could go back to the lovely-mannered Rick.

She phoned her stepfather's secretary, only to learn that he was going to be tied up all day. The secretary might be able to give Eliza a few minutes as soon as he got off the phone, if she cared to wait. She waited.

Charles Cummings fancied himself an art collector, but he was honest enough to admit that first and foremost he considered art an investment. Eliza was confident that she could convince him that the value of Michael's paintings would increase dramatically over the next decade—or even sooner.

When Charles came on the line, Eliza described Michael's landscapes. She ended by saying, "Have I ever given you bad advice about what paintings to buy? Have any of the paintings I recommended lost their resale value?"

"No. I'm sure if I wanted to sell any of them, I'd make a more than satisfactory profit. What did you say the painter's name was?"

"Michael Yuma. I think the autumn landscape would be perfect for your lake cottage."

"Really?" After a moment's silence, Charles asked, "Where in the cottage do you visualize it hanging?"

"In your den. Or in the dining room if Mom has changed the wallpaper." She might be pushing it, but she added, "You know, I think she'd like the spring landscape in the bedroom."

"I'll stop at the gallery on the way home."

"Great. You won't regret buying a Michael Yuma painting or two. Their value will probably double in the next decade or so. And in the meantime, you can enjoy them."

Eliza started to put the phone back into her purse but changed her mind. She dialed. The director of Charities, Inc. was in and could spare a few minutes to see Eliza.

"Walk with me to the storeroom," Kate Bailey said. "We can talk on the way." Kate looked at Eliza. "Wait a minute . . . aren't you supposed to be on vacation?"

"I changed my mind. Something came up." Deciding to plunge right in, Eliza asked, "is that assistant job you mentioned last week still open?"

"Yes. You interested?"

Eliza nodded.

"You know that job is different from the art project you've been doing as a volunteer."

"I know, but I still want to apply for it. What do I have to do?"

"Fill out an application . . . but we got all that information on you when you started as a volunteer worker. Then there'd be an interview with the director, which is me. We can skip that since I've known you for the past six months. So, the job is yours if you want it."

Eliza smiled broadly. "Thank you, thank you."

"Don't thank me too quickly. The job is hard. Working with troubled teenaged girls from dysfunctional families in a residential facility is no picnic. The salary is pitiful. The benefits, on the other hand, are quite decent. And since you live with your grandmother and won't have to pay rent, you'll manage to creep above the poverty level. I'm exaggerating, of course, but not by much."

"I'll be all right, Kate. Really. Thanks again."

"You're welcome. How soon can you start?"

"Next Monday."

"I wish it were today, but I understand that you'll need some time. Welcome aboard." Kate shook Eliza's hand before she went into the storeroom to check food supplies.

Eliza hurried outside where she could not restrain herself from raising her arm and semi-shouting a triumphant, "Yes!" Thank heaven no one saw her. Stopping beside her truck, she thought of Michael and sighed. She would not see him today because the clothes she was supposed to model had not arrived. She phoned the studio on the off chance that they might have arrived by special messenger.

"Hi, Michael. I'm just checking to see if the shipment came in."

"No such luck. We'll have to do double shoots the rest of the week to catch up with our schedule. We'll pay overtime, of course. You up for that?"

"Sure. You can count on me."

"Good. What are you doing with your free day?"

"First I'm cruising the second-hand stores for stuff for the apartment. And at 6:00 the team I help coach has soccer practice. I need to go and lead the workout."

"Soccer, huh? You're full of surprises. Where does your team practice?"

"In the field behind St. Anne's School. Are you a soccer player?" she asked.

"Uh-huh. When I was in fifth grade we got a new teacher on the rez from somewhere back east. He started a soccer team, and I played until I graduated from high school."

"Now it's my turn to say that you're full of surprises. What position did you play?"

"Mostly halfback."

"Me, too!" Eliza exclaimed.

"Midfield's the place to be for the best action."

What an astonishing coincidence. She and Michael had been separated geographically by half a continent and socio-economically by several layers, and yet they had things in common. A passion for art. A love for a sport. Not a bad beginning.

Eliza thought for a moment before she made a momentous decision. She was not sure how much overtime could cost the studio, but from remarks she had overheard, finances were stretched to the limit. Michael and John could use any small financial break they could get.

"I'll make you a deal. You come and help me coach the girls tonight, and you won't have to pay me overtime." In the silence that followed, Eliza held her breath. The silence grew until she wondered if she had broken some unwritten rule by suggesting he help her coach.

"Six o'clock? By then the optimum painting light is gone. You've got an assistant."

Pent up air rushed from Eliza's lungs. She took a controlling breath before she spoke. "Great. I'll see you then."

Eliza took a couple of quick dance steps. Suddenly the eternal honking of Chicago's taxis was not annoying. And the heat and humidity not so oppressive. She hopped into her truck and turned on the radio pushing the select button until she recognized the sweetly twangy voice of the singer. Enthusiastically, though without the twang, she sang along with Reba.

Michael spotted Eliza the moment he arrived at the soccer field. She had put her hair in a ponytail and wore a Cubs baseball cap that lent her a rakish air. He smiled as he approached her.

"Let me help you," he said, looking at the equipment on her truck. She turned to look at him with a smile that lit up her eyes.

"Hi. I'm glad you came."

"Did you think I wouldn't?"

"I wasn't sure. Coming to soccer practice on a hot

Chicago summer evening isn't exactly everybody's idea of fun." She paused, her expression serious. "After we spoke, it occurred to me that maybe I backed you into a corner and you were too nice to say no. I didn't mean to do that."

"I'm not easily backed into a corner," Michael told her. "And I have no trouble saying no." He grabbed a stack of orange cones and unloaded them. Eliza's observation wasn't far from the truth in one respect, though. Part of him did resent having agreed to come. It had nothing to do with his being too nice, but rather with his being too attracted to her. At the studio he could concentrate on the camera. He could view her in terms of the shot, of how the clothes looked on her. Here he had no choice but to regard her as a woman— a sexy, desirable woman.

He glanced at her surreptitiously as they unloaded the truck. This was the first time he'd seen her in shorts, and even with shin guards stuffed into her white knee socks, he could tell she had great legs—terrific, well-muscled thighs, and smooth, tanned skin. The hot afternoon suddenly got hotter.

What was the matter with him? He had no time for women. Painting had to be his exclusive focus until after the show. Even if he had time, Eliza was off limits. He paused, startled, trying to figure out why he thought this and suddenly he knew. She reminded him of all those popular, privileged girls in high school— the ones with the perfect teeth, glowing skin, and glossy hair that spoke of a lifetime of good nutrition and expensive medical and dental care. All those girls had looked at him as if he were invisible. Or if they had seen him, they had categorized him as part of the poor, wild Indian crowd they had been warned against by their mothers.

Occasionally one of the girls would come slumming, to see what the forbidden fruit felt and tasted like. But after a few furtive dates, they would hightail it back to their safe middle-class world with their curiosity satisfied. They never asked, much less cared, what chaos and confusion their brief descent into his world had caused. Briskly he dismissed the unpleasant memories though he never allowed himself to forget them.

Here in just three weeks he could hole up in his studio and do nothing but paint. He had dreamed of it, hungered for it, worked toward it since he had been eighteen years old. Nothing and no one would be allowed to derail him.

When he had unloaded the truck, Michael asked, "What do you want me to do next?"

"Would you mind setting up the cones for dribbling practice on the southern half of the field?"

Michael pulled his sunglasses down to look at Eliza. "Dribbling practice. Man, does that bring back the memories."

She grinned at him. "Your favorite, too?"

He grunted and pushed his glasses back up. "You want me to put the girls through the drill?"

"If you don't mind?"

"I don't, but they'll probably grumble."

"Too bad for them. If you'd seen their last game, you'd agree that they need the practice." Eliza tossed

him a whistle. "I'll take half of them and practice passing at the north end of the field. Then we'll switch
groups."

"Okay." Michael picked up a couple of cones.

"And Michael, don't be too easy on them. Their regular coach will be gone for a month, so the girls' parents have been taking turns overseeing practice. It's
great, but judging by the last game, the practices must
have been half-hearted at best."

"Aye, aye, captain. I'll be tough."

Eliza glanced at the edge of the field nearest the
parking lot. "Looks like they're all here. Let's start."

She blew her whistle and motioned the girls onto the
field. Before Michael left to set up the cones, Eliza
introduced him to the players. In the manner of twelve-
year olds, some greeted him shyly, some boldly, some
with giggles.

"Eliza, what are we doing today?" Brittany asked.

"Drills, drills, and more drills."

Loud moans and groans greeted her announcement.

"But we won our last game," Ashley pointed out.

Eliza nodded, "You did, but did you see the video of
the game that Brittany's father taped?" When they nodded, she asked, "Do you think you played a good
game?" All sixteen girls looked at the ground. Some
shifted their weight, some adjusted their knee pads,
some merely fidgeted.

"But we won," Ashley repeated, though her voice
was subdued.

"Yes, you won, by one goal against the weakest team
in the league." Eliza paused. "However, that's in the

past, and we won't dwell on it or assign blame." She could sense their relief. "Next Saturday, though, there will be no sloppy dribbling, no wussy, half-hearted passes, no wild shots at the goal. We'll play with control. We'll play with everything we've got. Now, let's get warmed up."

Eliza led the girls in stretching exercises that loosened every major muscle group of the body, and a warm-up lap around the field. Only then did they begin the drills.

From time to time Eliza allowed herself to look at the other half of the field to see if the dribbling drill was proceeding satisfactorily. *Yeah, right.* More likely it was to feast her eyes on Michael.

Demonstrating some fancy footwork, he was a picture of masculine grace, strength, and agility. Why had she not been born with sufficient talent to capture his beauty on canvas? Or in stone or bronze? She would gladly have traded her wealth and social position for a touch of that magical something that elevated the craftsman to artist.

Eliza seethed with frustration. The best she could hope for was an existence at the periphery of the artist's world. *At the edge of Michael's world? Oh yes!* She admired him as an artist. And as a man, he made her heart race and her palms grow damp every time she looked at him—or even thought about him. Imagining his strong arms around her, his voice murmuring soft words in her ears, his lips brushing hers—

"Eliza? Eliza? Am I doing this right?"

Torn out of the sensual daydream that had ensnared

her, Eliza blinked and brought her attention back to the
drill.

Ninety sweat-soaked minutes later, Eliza blew the
whistle to signal the end of practice. Michael felt like
collapsing on the ground, but Eliza segued into a series
of cool-down stretches. Tomorrow his body would
probably thank him, but now all he wanted was to lie
down and die. And he had thought that his daily jog-
ging had kept him in shape!

The girls helped pick up the equipment and load it on
the truck. From the cooler, Eliza handed out bottles of
cold water.

"Good practice, girls. Thanks."

Michael watched the girls beam with pleasure. It was
obvious that they adored Eliza even though she had put
them through their paces.

"Don't forget: eat your veggies and fruits, drink your
milk, and skip the junk food. I'll see you Thursday, at
the same time," Eliza said.

When the girls headed toward their parents' cars,
Eliza took off her cap and wiped her arm across her
damp forehead. She handed a quart bottle of water to
Michael and took one for herself.

"There's nothing as delicious as water," she murmured after quenching her thirst. She poured the water
over her shoulders and down the front of her T-shirt.
She closed her eyes in pleasure.

Imitating her, Michael upended the water bottle over
his head, enjoying the relief.

"Feels good, doesn't it?" Eliza asked with a smile.

She took the last bottle from the cooler and handed it to Michael.

He took a hefty swig before handing it back. Astonished, he watched Eliza raise it to her mouth without wiping it. Did she have any idea how intimate and trusting a gesture this was? Intently, hungrily, he saw her mouth where his had been moments earlier. This was almost like a kiss. He wanted to lean forward and kiss Eliza's lush mouth, but he stopped himself at the last moment. He could not trust himself not to keel over if he kissed her.

"Do you know what I have in my refrigerator?" Eliza asked. "A half gallon of homemade lemonade. Ice cold. A little on the tart side, so that it's more thirst quenching, but if you like it sweeter, we can add sugar."

"Are you inviting me over?" Michael asked.

"Yes. You were a great help with the girls. Offering you some nourishment is the least I can do."

Nourishment? Had she any idea what kind of nourishment he craved? Looking at her intently, he concluded that Eliza's words carried no double meaning, unfortunately. The invitation was innocent and straightforward. Like Eliza herself.

"You like lemonade?" she asked.

"Love it. Especially if it's on the tart side."

"There's also a big bowl of pasta salad. After the workout on the soccer field, you must be hungry."

"Pasta salad?"

From the way he said the word, Eliza guessed he was not fond of the dish. "This is not your usual mayonnaise-clogged pasta salad. It's not just noodles," she assured him.

Michael grinned at her. "I shouldn't think so. Not after what you told the girls about veggies and junk food."

Eliza blew at the strand of hair that had escaped her ponytail and fallen against her cheek. She assumed a mock-serious tone. "I'll have you know that this pasta salad contains at least six different vegetables as well as grilled chicken. And the whole thing is lightly tossed with a delicate vinaigrette. Even if you don't usually like pasta salad, you'll like this one."

She paused, waiting for Michael's reply. Fearing he might turn down her invitation, she added, "I also bought two wooden chairs today. I don't have a table yet, but you won't have to sit on the floor."

"That does it. How can I turn down an invitation that not only includes mouthwatering food and drink, but a chair to sit on?"

"Then you'll come?"

"Give me ten, fifteen minutes to shower, and I'll be there."

"Make it fifteen. I need to shower, too." Eliza smiled at him.

Michael reached out to tuck that errant strand of golden brown hair behind her ear. Eliza did not pull back or flinch. She met his gaze. He felt the silkiness of her hair, the heat of her body, the sweetness of her glance. He felt as if he teetered at the edge of an unknown territory that held both undreamed pleasure and unimagined danger.

Chapter Four

Dressed in a robe, Eliza stood at the studio window, looking out at the street. Winona had finished Eliza's hair and makeup. All they now needed was the shipment of clothes.

"Watching the street isn't going to get that truck here any sooner," John said.

"I know, but I hate waiting around."

"Why don't you come over here and tell me what you think."

Eliza sat beside him. John passed her the pages of the catalogue that he had laid out so far.

"Nice, very nice. I'm impressed," she said.

"Read the copy and tell me if anything strikes you as not quite right."

Eliza looked at the pages again, this time carefully reading the caption under each image. "I think the text has to be more descriptive. More specific, especially about the colors."

"Give me a for instance," John suggested.

"Okay. You describe this dress as red. As I recall, the color reminded me of a rich merlot."

John scratched his head. "Merlot?"

"Maybe merlot is too fancy, but you could say wine red or burgundy. I can wear that shade of red, but if the dress is crimson, forget it. Believe me, being specific will be very helpful to your customers."

"I see what you mean. Any other descriptions that need fixing?"

"Yes. You use brown several times. It's a bit boring and unappealing and not very specific. You could say walnut or oak or chocolate or cinnamon or cognac, just to name a few. And there are other colors. I could pencil in alternatives if you like."

"I'd appreciate that."

The phone rang. John leaped to answer it.

The door opened at the same time and Eliza looked up expectantly. "Oh, it's you," she said.

"Such enthusiasm. Should I go back out and come in again?" Michael asked with a raised eyebrow.

"I'm sorry. I was hoping it was the delivery guy."

"The shipment still hasn't come?"

"It's almost here," John said. "That was the head honcho of the trucking company telling me that the truck is on the Eisenhower Expressway and should be here within the hour."

"Good. Did he say why it didn't get here yesterday?"

"Some screwup in their office."

"So, it wasn't the women on the rez," Michael said, his voice expressing relief.

"You suspected your mom might have messed up? Cousin, what were you thinking?" John shook his head, making his ponytail whip from side to side.

"Yeah, what was I thinking," Michael said, his expression sheepish.

"Anyway, the head honcho swore there wouldn't be anymore delays. To pacify us, he isn't going to charge us for this delivery. That's not bad, huh?" John asked.

"It'll help the budget. I better go and set up the shoot."

Eliza watched him leave. "You've known Michael a long time?" she asked John.

"Uh-huh. We grew up on the same rez, went to the same schools, and enlisted in the military together."

"You were in the military?"

"You sound surprised."

"I am," Eliza said. "You're both so creative. I think of the military as just the opposite. You know, action versus creativity."

John shrugged, "Doing the military thing was the only way us boys from the rez could go to college."

Eliza started to say something, then closed her mouth. There was no sense in revealing her ignorance. She had been only vaguely aware that the military was the way many Americans got a college education. How poor people were educated had not been a dinner conversation at her mother's table, or at the private schools she had attended.

"Do you know Michael's mother?" Eliza asked.

"Yes, and she's one smart, strong lady. Figured out how to make clothes by learning to do alterations. You know, take a dress apart to fix the shoulder line, take in a dart, or let out the waist. That's the way you learn how the dress was put together in the first place. She supported the two of them by doing alterations for a department store in town."

"Is that how you got interested in designing clothes?"

"Uh-huh. I spent more time at Michael's house than my own. At my place we were seven, so it was always loud and crowded. At Michael's it was just him and his mom."

Eliza wondered if Michael's parents were divorced like her own, but decided that this was not a question she should ask John.

"Anyway, I used to watch his mom work. Pretty soon I was helping her with the alterations." He chuckled, "For a while that earned me a lot of black eyes."

"You got into fights?"

"Sure did. You know how kids are. I got teased a lot."

"But that didn't stop you. And Michael wasn't interested in helping?"

"Nah. He liked soccer and baseball and filling notebooks with drawings."

"And girls?"

John grinned. "We both liked girls. Only he didn't have to chase them. They chased him."

Eliza had no trouble believing that. "So, whose idea

was it to start this catalogue and online clothing business?"

"We worked it out together, but initially it was Michael's idea. The department store's a long way from the rez and Dakota winters aren't exactly mild. He worried about his mom driving that far in bad weather. Especially as she's getting older."

Eliza felt a tightness in her throat. What a loving, caring thing to do. No wonder she admired and liked Michael so much. "I don't suppose you learned clothing design in the army?"

John laughed. "Not exactly. They thought since we were Indians we'd be good at tracking, so they made us cops."

"Military police?" Eliza asked, her voice incredulous.

"Yup. Another guy who enlisted with us scored high on the math test, so they made him a cook. Who understands the white man's ways?" John asked, and winked.

Eliza was spared a reply as the truck with the clothes arrived.

They worked long, tiring hours, but by the middle of the third day, the shoot was finished. John dismissed the models with thanks.

Although Eliza had known that the modeling gig would come to an end, she still felt a letdown.

"Eliza, can I see you for a minute?" Michael called to her from the dark room.

"Sure," she said, wondering what he wanted. She had had to give up coaching because of her new job, and she had been racking her brain trying to think of some way to continue to be with Michael. She could not imagine not seeing him again.

"Yes, Michael?"

"My mom is sending one more shipment of clothes. It's a small one. Only eight or nine outfits. Would you be interested in modeling those?"

"I'd love to," she said with a smile. She hoped she did not sound too eager. Then she remembered her job, and her smile faded.

"Is there a problem?"

"I told you I'll be starting a new job on Monday. My hours will be a lot less flexible."

"You have weekends off?"

"Sundays and every other Saturday."

"That'll work." Michael watched a smile light up her face. She had taken off the heavy makeup she had worn for the shoot. Her porcelain skin glowed with health and vitality. He loved what light did to it.

He would have to paint her. Otherwise her expressive, lovely face would haunt him. That meant he would have to continue to see her, to win her trust. Though he was not going to ask her to pose nude, he did want to paint her in a pose that revealed some of that beautiful skin. Perhaps draped with a silk shawl, the color of purple irises or deep pink phlox.

He had noticed that Eliza was modest. The other models had changed clothes in back of the room, not minding whether he or John saw them wearing only panties and bras. But not Eliza. She had always stepped behind the screen to change.

"Hey, Cuz. Phone call," John yelled across the room.

"Excuse me, Eliza."

She watched him walk across the floor. Did Michael know that she observed him whenever she had the chance? She hoped not. She usually tried to focus on something else, but more often than not failed. Her eyes seemed to have a mind of their own, wanting to gaze at nothing but him.

Michael stood near a window. The light brought out the bluish undertones of his black hair which he always wore tied back. Eliza had never seen it loose but knew if she ever got a chance to touch it, it would feel thick, rich, alive in her hands.

"What's the matter?" John asked when Michael replaced the phone. "You look sort of pole-axed."

"The gallery. They sold all of my paintings—all four. I can hardly believe it." He sat down heavily in the nearest chair.

The gallery had taken its time notifying Michael of the sales, Eliza reflected resentfully.

Michael and John exchanged high fives.

"Winona, did you hear that?" John yelled, hurrying toward the office.

"Congratulations, Michael. That's wonderful," Eliza said. When he hugged her, she felt a moment of unease. What would his reaction be when he found out she had been instrumental in selling his paintings? Well, she had been responsible for the sale of only three of them. Someone else bought the spring landscape. It was not all her doing, she rationalized. Dismissing the niggling thoughts, she let herself enjoy the feeling of Michael's arms around her.

His denim shirt smelled of paint, which told her that he had spent time at the easel that morning. Eliza loved the smell of paint.

Winona's arrival ended the embrace.

"This calls for a celebration," Eliza said. "I'm going to the corner bakery and get the most sinfully delicious cake they have. What's your favorite, Michael?"

He shrugged and smiled. "Any kind. You choose."

"I'll make a fresh pot of coffee," Winona offered. "It should be ready by the time you get back."

And it was. Winona had set out mugs, milk, sugar, plates and forks.

"What did you get?" Winona asked eagerly.

"I couldn't make up my mind. They all looked good to me, so I got an assortment." Carefully she lifted the cake slices from the white carton onto a plate. "Here we have two pieces of dark chocolate layer cake, two German chocolate, two cheese cakes, one carrot and one coconut."

Michael chose cheesecake. Eliza made a mental note to get her grandmother's recipe and practice until she could whip up a cheesecake that was equal to the bakery's.

While they ate, their conversation revolved around Michael's paintings.

"Do you have a couple of paintings to replace those sold by the gallery?" Eliza asked, "Or are you saving all of them for your show?"

Michael thought for a few seconds before replying. "I could take one from the rodeo series and one of the powwow dancers."

"Good," Eliza said. "You need to call the gallery immediately to let them know you have more paintings. If word-of-mouth recommendations work the way they usually do, people are going to see your painting in someone's home, like it, ask where it was bought, go to the gallery—"

Michael and John exchanged a look that stopped Eliza. "What?" Her gaze flicked from one man to the other. "Oh . . . I'm telling you what to do. I don't mean to. I get carried away. I'm sorry."

"Don't be sorry," Michael said. "I like your enthusiasm. I'm just wondering if selling my paintings is really that simple."

"It's supply and demand. Right now your paintings are coming into demand. You need to get the right people to see them."

"And who are the right people?" Michael asked, intrigued.

"The ones who can afford to buy them. Maybe that sounds crass, but it's not enough for people to like your paintings. They have to have the means to buy them. And I think you should ask more money for your paintings."

Michael looked skeptical; John interested.

"You might as well, because I'm sure the gallery will jack up the price. That's what happens when a product starts to sell." Hastily she added, "Not that your paintings are products in the sense that ratchets or mufflers or kitchen sinks are products."

"What Eliza says makes sense," John said, with an approving voice. "Have you ever worked in sales or manufacturing?" When Eliza shook her head, he asked, "Your family maybe?"

"Both my dad and brother work in banks."

"I bet they don't work as tellers," Michael said.

"Not now, but when they started, they each had to do a stint in a teller's cage," Eliza said a little defensively. *Was that a note of irony in Michael's voice? Resentment? A little of each? Maybe her grandmother was right and she should tell Michael all about her family's wealth.*

No. She might lose him before they'd had a chance to find out if this relationship could blossom into something more. Or alternatively, Michael could suddenly become exceedingly interested in her because of her family's status. It had happened before. Though she did not think that Michael was mercenary, everybody was at least a little bit impressed by wealth. She could not tell him yet. Eliza wanted a chance to win him on her own merits. John's voice broke into her thoughts.

"What do they do now?" John wanted to know. "Your dad and your brother."

"Dad's in administration."—which was true to a certain degree—"And Peter is a loan officer. He specializes in loans to small businesses. If Sun Designs needs a loan, I'd recommend you see him. Peter is really good at his job."

"Thanks," John said, "we may have to do that."

"You never said what your new job was. Is it in banking?" Michael asked.

"Heaven forbid! Two members of the family talking

at dinner about mortgages and loans, and speculating if the Fed is going to raise or lower interest rates, is quite enough."

"Then what is your new job?" Winona asked.

"I'm an assistant counselor at a shelter for teenaged girls."

"Wow. Seems to me working in a bank would be a lot easier than dealing with teenagers," Winona said.

"Probably," Eliza shrugged, "but it appeals to me more than banking." She looked at her watch. "Speaking of the shelter, I have to attend a training session."

"I'll walk you to your truck," Michael offered. Accompanying her, he asked, "What hours do you work?"

"I have the graveyard shift."

Michael stopped walking. "Did you choose that shift?"

"No. It was the only one available. I guess it's the least popular, but I don't mind. I don't have any trouble sleeping during the day, once I adjust. I'll probably stay up till noon and then go to bed. When your mom's shipment arrives, I could model the clothes in the morning."

"That'll work." Michael walked her the rest of the way to her truck. "You mentioned your dad and your brother. What about your mom? Is she a housewife?"

Trying to envision her mother in that role, Eliza stopped in her tracks. "A housewife?" After a lengthy pause, she added, "I suppose so . . . Sort of . . . I mean she isn't a career woman. But she also isn't the type who bakes cookies, knits sweaters, or makes bread from scratch."

When they reached the truck, Eliza unlocked it. Turning to face Michael, she said, "You've talked about your mom but not about your dad."

"That's because I don't know the man. He walked out on us when I was three years old." Michael opened the truck's door for her. "I'll let you know when the shipment arrives. Drive carefully."

Eliza hesitated, wanting to wipe away the grim look on Michael's face and the hard expression in his beautiful black eyes that the mention of his father had put there, but she did not know how to do that. So she merely nodded.

"Give me a call, please." Not wanting him to think she was being pushy, or wanting him to call her for a date even though she wanted precisely that, she added, "When the clothes arrive."

During the following week Eliza waited for Michael's call. When it came, it left her momentarily speechless.

"Eliza, did you hear me?"

"Um, yes. You said you wanted me to come to your studio?"

"I told you I'd give you a tour of the place."

"Yes, you did. I'm glad you remembered." Eliza raised her hand in a silent victory salute.

"Does that mean you'll come?"

"Of course. When?" She sounded like an over-eager teenager.

"Tomorrow morning after your shift ends?"

"Okay."

Michael gave her his address. "You can tell me all about your new job."

When Eliza arrived at Michael's studio the next morning, he could tell something was troubling her.

"You look upset." He reached for her hand and pulled her into the area of the loft that served as a living room. "Something go wrong at the shelter?" he asked.

"You could say that," Eliza said and collapsed on the couch he indicated. "One of the girls, Brandy, ran away during the night. Out the upstairs window and down the drainpipe."

"Good grief. Lucky the drainpipe didn't bust and send her crashing to the ground."

"The only reason it didn't is because Brandy is as thin as an exclamation point." Eliza took a shuddering breath. "If she'd fallen she could have broken a leg or injured her spine and be crippled for the rest of her life. Why would she risk that?"

"Maybe she wanted to see her folks?"

"She doesn't have any. I mean she does have a mother, but she's in a clinic getting dried out and her father hasn't been around for years. Nobody knows where he is. The grandparents live in a small town downstate and declined to take her. So where was she going at midnight?"

"Looking for friends? A party? Getting out on the street?"

"She's only fourteen!"

Eliza was near tears. Michael took her hand in his

and pressed it reassuringly. "Doesn't that say it all? Most fourteen-year-olds have little common sense. They don't think of the consequences of what they do."

"I know."

"Can I get you something? Coffee?"

"I've been drinking coffee all night long. I'm so wired I may never sleep again."

"A glass of milk?" When she nodded he poured her a glass. "Drink this. It's soothing." He waited until she took several sips before he sat beside her. "Tell me about the shelter. Doesn't it have a security system?"

"Only on the downstairs doors."

"Eliza, it's not your fault that Brandy ran. You couldn't watch all the girls simultaneously."

"Nobody's blaming me. Girls run away all the time, but that doesn't make it any less scary. It doesn't make me feel less guilty."

"How'd you find out she was missing?"

"I do a bed check every hour. She was in bed at eleven and gone at twelve."

"What did you do when you found her missing?"

"After I managed to control my panic, I followed standard procedures."

"Which are?"

Eliza used her fingers to tick off the steps. "Called the police and reported a runaway. Filled out the form which an officer picked up half an hour later. I entered the incident in the log. And then I did my usual chores."

"And what are those?"

"Michael, do you really want to know that or are you just being nice?"

"I'm interested," he said and tried to push a strand of her hair back into the rubber band that held her ponytail in place.

Eliza reached up, trying to help him. "It's no use," she muttered. She freed her hair and shook it.

Michael lifted her hair, letting it fall through his fingers, enjoying the silken texture, watching the sunshine from the window highlighting it. "I bet your hair is at least half a dozen different shades of gold and brown. The whole autumn palette. It's going to be a joy and a challenge."

"It is? I don't understand."

"When I paint it. When I paint you. I'm going to, you know."

"I didn't know," Eliza murmured, her surprise and anticipation fighting for first place.

"Will you pose for me?"

"Depends."

"On what? I didn't say I wanted to paint you nude." *Liar.* Of course, he did. No painter alive wouldn't want to paint her nude. The beauty of women's bodies had been the favorite subject of painters since—

"I hadn't even considered that possibility," Eliza said, her breath suddenly fluttery. "I was actually wondering if I'd end up with one eye on my forehead, no nose, and a lopsided mouth."

Michael chuckled, "I admire Picasso but I won't imitate him. I'll paint you in a realist mode." Michael moved back a fraction so he could study her better. "With flowers, I think."

"When did it occur to you to paint me?"

"The moment I took a good look at you I knew you'd be a great subject. Just as you were a great photo model." Michael kept playing with Eliza's hair, pulling it back, piling it on top of her head, fluffing it around her face.

"Michael, what are you doing?"

Enjoying your glorious hair. Aloud he said, "Trying to figure out which way I want you to wear your hair when I paint you. How soon can you pose?"

"You're serious?"

"Dead serious. I'd love for you to pose for me right after you get through at the shelter. The morning light is best. I'll pay you, of course."

Eliza was speechless. To be immortalized in one of Michael's paintings was nothing she would ever have dared to dream. She felt like she ought to pay *him,* but knew better than to suggest that.

"You don't have to pay me." Seeing his expression, she added quickly, "At least not until you sell more paintings. After your show."

"That doesn't seem right."

"It's fine. We'll keep track of the hours I sit for you."

"If you're sure . . ."

"I am." Eliza glanced at her watch. "I wonder if they've found my runaway yet."

"You want to call the shelter? The phone's over there," he said, pointing.

"Thanks." Eliza dialed the shelter.

After she had listened for a few seconds, Michael saw her close her eyes and lean against the table.

Chapter Five

When Michael rushed to Eliza's side, she smiled and gave him the thumbs-up sign. From her stance he could see the tension drain from her body. She did not seem to mind his standing close to her and listening to her side of the conversation.

"Where did the cops find her?" she asked.

He watched her eyes widen.

"That's not exactly Chicago's safest neighborhood. Brandy's lucky she wasn't attacked. Or worse." Eliza shook her head. "What was she doing there?" After a couple of seconds she said, her voice disbelieving, "Hanging out? At night, in that area? I don't even want to know who she was hanging out with."

Eliza talked a bit longer and then hung up. She turned toward Michael, her expression thoughtful.

"So, what'll happen to Brandy for pulling this stunt?" Michael wanted to know.

"Nothing much, except she'll get a good tongue-lashing and lecture from the director."

"That's all?"

"The shelter's not a prison. We're limited as to what we can do. We could ground her from our next outing, but we don't have sufficient staff to leave someone at the shelter with her. Deprive her of dessert? I suspect she's got food issues as it is, so that would be counterproductive."

"Food issues? Like an eating disorder?" Michael asked.

"That's what I suspect."

Michael shook his head. "We didn't always have enough food on the rez, so I don't understand someone deliberately starving themselves."

"You sound just like my grandmother," Eliza said with a smile. Then sobering, she added, "I think Brandy's food issues are about control. Right now her body is the only thing in her life that she has any control over." Eliza shrugged. "I'm not an expert on eating disorders, so that's only a guess."

"What are you going to do to keep her from running away again? What *can* you do?"

"Move her to a different room. One from which she can't reach the drainpipe. Talk to her and listen if she feels like confiding in me."

Michael looked at Eliza with awe. He could not imagine anyone deliberately choosing to deal with a lot of screwed-up teenagers. "I agree with Winona. Working in a bank has to be easier."

"I'm sure it is," Eliza agreed with a shrug, "But enough about the shelter and my problems. Didn't you promise me a tour of your studio? And a look at your paintings?"

Michael smiled at the eagerness in her soft voice and the light in her lovely eyes. "There aren't that many paintings yet. You can help me decide which two to take to the gallery. The owner is suddenly eager to show a couple more of my paintings. You were right about that," he admitted.

Eliza grinned at him.

"No 'I told you so,'?" he asked.

"I hate it when someone says that to me."

"Yeah, me too." Michael placed his hand lightly on the small of her back and led her past a bookcase and a particle board partition that served as a bulletin board for sketches. When her step slowed as if she wanted to stop to look at the drawings, he urged her on with slight pressure from his hand.

"This is it." He tried to look at his work area through Eliza's eyes. Would she see merely a large messy space, with a paint-spattered table, canvases stacked against the walls, a camera setup with lights?

"This is great," Eliza exclaimed. "It's exactly the kind of studio I'd want if I'd been blessed with real talent."

Michael chided himself for not remembering that Eliza had studied art. She would appreciate the strategically-placed windows, the ample space, the—

"Do you photograph your subjects before you paint them?" she asked, indicating the camera.

"Sometimes . . . It depends on the subject. Landscapes I photograph because it's a lot easier to work in the studio than outdoors. Animals too because they don't sit still long enough, except maybe a cat taking a nap."

"You like cats?"

The way she asked the question, Michael knew the answer was important to her. "Sure. Why?"

"I just wondered."

"Are you thinking of getting one?"

"I'm thinking about it, but I don't know if the cat is. I've been putting food and water on the fire escape for him and leaving the window open for a while each day, but so far he hasn't come in. The super said somebody moved away and abandoned him. Can you imagine doing that to a pet?"

He saw indignation on Eliza's face and tears in her eyes. How softhearted and innocent she was in some ways. *If people could abandon their children, what would keep them from leaving an animal?* Michael could not help but wonder. Aloud he said, "As soon as it gets cold, he'll take you up on your invitation. Maybe even sooner."

"Do you think so?" she asked eagerly.

"Yes. Why wouldn't he want to move in with you?" *I would. Hold it, Yuma!* What was the matter with him? Hadn't he sworn off women for the next six months while he concentrated single-mindedly on his painting? Michael hardened his heart. Eliza would be his model. That would be enough—it would have to be.

After a thoughtful silence, Eliza said, "I hope you're right about the cat. He's gorgeous, with smoke-gray and white fur, big white paws, and yellow eyes. He pads across the fire escape as though he owned it." She paused again. "I wonder if you'd use sienna or ochre for his eyes if you painted him."

"Either, with a touch of umber. Are you hiring me to paint a portrait of your cat?"

"He isn't even my cat yet, and I strongly suspect he would sit for you only if and when it suited him."

"The independent type, huh?"

"Like you."

Michael grinned. He followed her as she walked to the table and touched the different items on it. She seemed to touch the objects reverently, lovingly. He surely wouldn't mind if she touched him like that. *Don't go there,* he warned himself.

"Oil, watercolor, acrylic, and guache? You use all four?"

"A different medium for a different mood or subject."

"Then you're even more talented than I thought you were."

"Come and be the judge." Michael walked to the far wall. He picked up the nearest canvas and turned it so she could see it. He continued until they were all facing her.

"The first four are the best I did of the rodeo series. The next two are dancers from a powwow. Then there are two landscapes and a still life."

Eliza hunkered down in front of each painting and took her time looking at them.

Does she like what she sees? he wondered. *What is she thinking? And why does it matter so much what she thinks?* Yet her opinion mattered more to him than that of a critic, a gallery owner, or a potential buyer—more than all of them combined. *This is not good.*

When she reached the last painting, she walked back slowly, her eyes still on the canvases.

"Well?" he demanded, his voice slightly edgy.

Surprised by his tone, she looked at him. "You don't need me to tell you how good these are."

"No, but it would be nice to hear it anyway. You took such a long time looking."

"I was trying to decide which I'd recommend you take to the gallery. Isn't that what you wanted me to do?"

"It is."

"And that decision isn't one that can be made hastily."

"I agree. Which do you like best?"

"That's the problem. I like them all."

"You do?" Michael felt a warm rush of pure pleasure surge through him.

"I do—every one. I've been to a rodeo only once. A small one, and what I remember was the heat, the sweat, the smell of the animals, the obvious adrenaline rush of the contestants as they hurtled out of the chutes. And, of course, the excitement of the crowd. You captured all of it in every one of these paintings."

Eliza moved on to the next two canvases. "I've never been to a powwow, but from the colors you used—these incredible reds, oranges and yellows—I can feel the beat of the drums and hear the pounding of the dancers' feet as they stomp the ground. It's amazing."

Michael followed her slowly, enjoying her reaction. Enjoying? He was lapping it up.

"Two winter landscapes. I can't decide which I like better—the one in bright sunshine with the sharp shadows and the glittering blue-white snow, or the evening scene. It's the same red barn in both, isn't it?" When Michael nodded, she said, "The evening scene has such a sense of serenity about it that it makes the viewer feel calm, too."

Eliza moved to the last canvas. "I'm a sucker for a good still life. And this one is good . . . so good," she murmured, her voice solemn. "How can such simple, everyday objects be so pleasing to the eye? I mean, there's just an old, dented, blue enamelware coffee pot, a matching mug, and a white plate with three oranges on it?"

"Tell me, why is it so pleasing to you?" Michael leaned down beside Eliza and looked at her expectantly.

"You didn't say there'd be a quiz!" she said with a smile.

Michael chuckled. He had never known a woman with whom he could discuss his work so easily—a woman who understood painting as a process and as a product. It was amazing.

"Well, let me see. The still life is good because of the way the objects are arranged. They're balanced, harmonious. And because of the colors, the different tones of blue complemented by orange. And because you've created just the right accent with the red stripes of the tablecloth." She looked at him for confirmation. "Am I close?"

"Very close. You'd make a good art teacher."

"I guess that's the second best thing if you can't be a painter." Eliza's gaze moved again from painting to painting. "You know, this makes me so mad I could scream."

Michael looked at her, both alarmed and puzzled. "What makes you so mad?"

"Your having to work construction and heaven only knows what else. You, a man with incredible talent, wasting your time doing menial jobs—time that should be spent painting."

He shrugged philosophically. "Those are the breaks unless you have rich parents."

"Or wealthy patrons the way they did during the Renaissance. If you had such a patron, or even a rich wife—"

"That would be great, but it isn't going to happen."

"The wealthy patron?"

". . . or the rich wife," he added.

Eliza opened her mouth and then snapped it shut quickly.

"What?" Michael asked.

"Nothing." Eliza averted her eyes. She had almost blown it by volunteering to become his patron.

When she made a move to stand, Michael jumped up and held out his hand to help her. He liked holding her hand. Heck, he liked touching her. Liked? He loved it. Realizing the forbidden direction his thoughts were taking, he let go of her hand.

"So, which two paintings do you recommend I take to the gallery?"

"The still life and one of the landscapes," she said without hesitation.

"Why?"

"Because you shouldn't break up the set of the rodeo or the powwow."

"That's what I thought, too."

Eliza seemed to be pondering something. Then,

apparently coming to a decision, she took two steps toward him. Quickly she cradled his face between her hands and kissed him on the mouth. For a split second Michael was paralyzed by surprise. Then a feeling so sweet that he thought he might faint flowed through him. When she released him abruptly, he almost staggered. Speechlessly he watched her walk toward the sofa where she had left her handbag.

He followed her. "What was that for?" he managed to ask, his voice a mere croak.

"For showing me your paintings. Thank you."

"You're welcome." He saw a mischievous look flit across her face.

"Have you heard the old line about a man showing a woman his etchings? There's definitely something to that."

Michael chuckled, "I'll have to remember that." When she picked up her bag, he said, "Don't go yet. I'd like to take a couple of photos to see how I'll pose you. Please."

"Since you asked so nicely, why not? Where do you want me to sit? Stand?"

"Stand." He dragged a small table in front of the camera. "I think I want you right here," he said, placing his hands on her shoulders and moving her gently behind the table. He felt the warmth of her body through the fabric of her blouse, felt it seep under his skin and warm him to the bone. *Stop touching her,* his mind commanded. Reluctantly his hands obeyed the order.

He moved behind the tripod. Looking at her through the camera, Michael studied the planes, the lines, the curves, the shadows of her arresting face. His hands itched to grab paper and charcoal and start drawing. *Not yet.* He took a calming breath.

"Move a little to your right. That's good. Stay there." Michael fetched a piece of chalk and drew a line in front of the table and in front of her feet to mark the position. He moved one of the floodlights a few inches and then took several photos. "Great," he murmured. "I know this is short notice, but can you come tomorrow morning?"

"Don't you have to finish your current work in progress?" she asked, nodding toward the cloth-covered easel.

"I'll finish that today. Can you come? I don't mean to be pushy, but I'm eager to start."

"I'll be here."

Michael smiled, "Good."

"What shall I wear?"

"Whatever you wore to work. I'll have something for you. You can change here." He saw her eyes light up with excitement.

"We're going to play dress-up? Rembrandt loved to dress his subjects in fancy outfits—even himself when he painted a self-portrait."

"I won't dress you in historical costume."

"What then?"

He smiled at her enthusiasm. "You'll just have to wait and see."

"You'll be ready to start when I get off work in the morning?"

He had been ready to paint her since the day he had followed her through the Art Institute. "I'll be ready."

"All right then."

Michael walked her to the door. He placed one hand against it to keep her from leaving. She looked at him with startled eyes. He still was not sure how he would capture their color on canvas, but that was a problem for another time. Right now he was hungry for one more taste of her sweet lips. He lifted her chin and kissed her gently, leisurely, carefully, and though he tried to keep his hunger from spiraling out of control, he did not entirely succeed. When he released Eliza, his heart pounded, his breathing was ragged.

"What was that for?" Eliza murmured, pressing the palms of her hands against the door behind her to steady herself.

"For looking at my paintings. Thanks."

"Any time."

Eliza opened the door and paused, seemingly uncertain what to do. Then she smiled. "See you tomorrow," she said and left.

Michael leaned against the closed door. Kissing Eliza was probably the dumbest thing he had done all week—all month! He smacked his hand against his forehead. "Stupid, stupid," he said aloud. Now every time he looked at her, he'd think of kissing her. But how could he have known that her kisses would leave him breathless and dazed? Distract him? Rob him of the single-minded dedication he needed for his work?

Just think of her as a subject. Planes and angles. Light and shadow. Hues and tints. Right. He had worked too hard and too long to be distracted now.

Once, when he had just started painting seriously, he

had let a woman ensnare him and almost allowed her to convince him to get a *real* job with a steady paycheck and give up the "ridiculous, unprofitable" idea of art. It would have killed his soul and driven him to drink and heaven knew what else. Michael shuddered, not wanting to think what would have become of him.

His shot at a one-man exhibition was within his grasp. Nothing could deter him, not even Eliza of the heady, knee-buckling kisses.

Eliza did not go home but drove straight to her grandmother's house. When she got there and saw her mother's car in the driveway, she was momentarily tempted to turn around and flee to her apartment. Why was her mother there? Ordinarily Gloria visited her mother-in-law only for major family celebrations that she thought showed bad form to miss. Had something happened to Hendrika?

Her heart pounding with anxiety, Eliza rushed into the house. Sturges met her in the foyer.

"Good morning, Miss Eliza. They're on the verandah," he said, anticipating her question.

"Thank you, Sturges." Eliza walked toward the back of the house. Pausing in the open doorway, she took in the scene. Hendrika, sitting in a chintz-covered wicker chair, was calmly working on her embroidery. Gloria, dressed in a coral linen dress accented by a simple string of perfectly-matched pearls, paced the length of the verandah. She carried a small ashtray into which she flicked the ashes from her cigarette. That was not a good sign. Usually her mother forced herself to wait to have her first cigarette with the one martini a day she allowed herself at happy hour.

"There you are," Hendrika said, looking up from her work.

"It's about time you came," Gloria said, making a show of looking at her watch.

"I didn't know I was supposed to be here at a certain time."

"You weren't," Hendrika assured her. "I told Gloria that you would probably come today to have breakfast with me after you got off work."

"You turned off your cell phone, didn't you?" Gloria asked, her tone accusatory.

"Yes," Eliza admitted, not adding that its ringing interrupted the painting sessions. "What happened that you had to see me so urgently?"

"A number of things, but foremost that ridiculous job of yours."

It was going to be one of *those* conversations. Eliza braced herself. She would not lose her temper. She would not. Calmly she said, "My job is not ridiculous. Low-paying, but definitely not ridiculous."

"It is ridiculous—totally ridiculous," Gloria stabbed her cigarette in a staccato movement to underscore her words. "You spend your time with maladjusted girls from the worst segments of society. With your background and education, that's not only ridiculous, it's ludicrous."

Eliza's gaze met her grandmother's who shook her head slightly. Her message was clear: *Don't get into a fight with Gloria. It would be pointless and upsetting.*

Eliza knew that. She sat on the couch, picked up one of her grandmother's small needlepoint pillows and hugged it to her chest.

"And what job should I get that wouldn't be ridiculous in your view?"

"Oh, for heaven's sake! If you have to have a job, work in your father's bank. Or continue to do appropriate volunteer work." Fixing Eliza with her skillfully made-up blue eyes that were glacier cold just then, she said, "I know from reliable sources that there are a number of suitable young men in our social circle who're interested in you. You could get married. You are old enough."

"And have a husband, or several of them, support me in luxury for the rest of my life?"

Eliza heard her grandmother's gasp and knew she'd gone too far. "Sorry, Mom. That was uncalled for."

"You think being the wife of a successful man is easy? It's not. You're on call twenty-four hours a day. You have to look perfect every minute, be interested and interesting, be gracious and accommodating whether you feel like it or not. You have to provide unstinting support, praise and loyalty. He and his needs come first in every way and all the time. You . . . ," Gloria's voice broke off.

The silence that followed Gloria's outburst seemed to freeze them in a stunned tableaux. Eliza thought her mother might be fighting back tears. Quietly she said, "I'm sorry, Mom. I didn't mean to upset you." Eliza paused. Then thoughtfully she added, "It seems to me putting in eight hours a day with maladjusted girls is a whole lot easier than being married to a successful man."

"Oh, it's not all that bad, of course," Gloria said, recovering her poise. "As a matter of fact, marriage has a lot going for it. I know Rick wants to marry you. He and I have talked about it. You'd be the perfect couple. I don't know what you're waiting for."

"That is *so* never going to happen. I'll never marry Rick." Eliza's voice, though soft, was laced with absolute certainty.

"And why not, all of a sudden? You've dated him on and off for several years. What's suddenly wrong with him?"

Eliza shrugged. "I never had anybody to compare him to."

"Now you have? Who?" Gloria demanded.

"Somebody I met. A painter." Eliza watched her mother's face go pale under the makeup.

"Oh no! That's my worst nightmare coming true!"

Eliza saw Hendrika and Gloria exchange a look she could not interpret.

"You've met some struggling would-be artist who's only interested in your money and how you're going to bankroll his career," Gloria said.

"Thank you for your confidence, Mom. He couldn't possibly be interested in me as a person, as a woman, could he?" Eliza heard the bitter tone in her voice. She had not meant to reveal how much her mother's words had hurt her.

"I didn't mean it that way. But you have to admit that money is awfully attractive."

And you would know. Eliza clamped her teeth together to keep from uttering the words out loud. When she had control of her voice, she said, "He doesn't know I have money."

"Well, that's something. Keep it that way." Gloria stubbed out her cigarette. "About Rick . . . don't rule him out. Don't make a hasty decision you'll regret." She picked up her purse. "Your stepfather's birthday is coming up. It would be nice if you could stop by."

"I'll try, Mom."

Gloria nodded to Hendrika and left.

"For a moment there I thought this might get ugly," Hendrika said. "I'm proud of you, darling. You kept your temper even when Gloria provoked and hurt you."

"Why does she always do that? Make me feel as though I were totally unlovable? That no man could possibly be interested in me for me alone?" Eliza bit her lower lip. The pain kept in check the tears that threatened to flood her eyes.

"She doesn't mean to. She just wants you to be perfect—her version of perfect."

"Reed thin and slavishly following the dictates of her social set?"

"Don't be so hard on her. She grew up as a poor relative of a prominent family. Poor because her mother married a man her parents considered unsuitable and they disinherited her. I'm sure Gloria felt, and possibly still feels, a little inferior because of that. She compensates by being as perfect an embodiment of the socialite wife as she can be."

Eliza stared at her grandmother. "Looking at her from that point of view, I can almost feel sorry for her."

"Don't feel sorry for her," Hendrika chided gently. "Understand her and make allowances."

"I guess I can do that. Maybe she'll even reciprocate—but I'm not holding my breath." Eliza paused for a beat. "Did you notice her reaction when I told her that Michael was a painter? What was that all about?"

"Let's go and have brunch."

"You're evading my question. There's a story here, isn't there? Tell me, please."

"It's not for me to tell. Ask your mother."

One look at Hendrika's face told Eliza that she would not get anything else out of her grandmother.

"Come and tell me about Michael's paintings while we eat."

"How did you know I saw his paintings?"

"Grandmothers know these things." Hendrika placed her arm around Eliza's waist. "Earlier this morning the heavenly smell of baking wafted from the kitchen. I suspect we're having cinnamon bread."

Chapter Six

Mentally, Eliza gritted her teeth. She had been holding the pose for so long her arms screamed for relief.

When she fidgeted slightly, Michael asked, "Do you need a break?"

"If you don't mind . . ."

"Of course I don't mind. You have to tell me when you get tired of holding a pose. Once I start painting I forget about everything else."

Eliza laid the deep pink phlox she had been holding on the little table in front of her. She rotated her shoulders and rolled her head from side to side.

Michael walked to the sink in the corner and washed his hands. "What time is it?"

"Almost eleven."

Michael stopped in the act of reaching for the towel. "What happened to the morning?"

"It flew by."

He shook his head with a frown. "I can't believe I made you stand there without moving for such a long time. I'm so sorry. Why didn't you yell at me to stop?"

"You were so into your work I didn't have the heart to interrupt you."

"You should have. From now on, I'll set a timer. A professional model would never have allowed me to paint that long without giving her a break. She'd have called me an inconsiderate brute or worse, and I'd have deserved it."

"But you got a lot done, didn't you?"

"Well, yes, but that's not the point. You—"

"Michael, that's exactly the point. Stop glowering. In the future I'll yell if my shoulder muscles start to scream."

"It's the angle in which you hold the flowers. Maybe I should paint you sitting down."

"No. I saw you use charcoal which means you've sketched the outlines. For you to change the composition now, would mean wasting almost three hours' worth of work. No way." Eliza folded her arms across her chest.

"Why Eliza Marshall! You've got a stubborn streak," Michael said, his voice surprised, his expression bemused.

"Doesn't everyone when it comes to something they care about, or if they're sure they're right?"

"A stubborn streak. Who'd have thought it," he said with a grin.

"That seems to amuse you. Why?"

"It shows that you're not a fairy-tale princess but a

flawed mortal like the rest of us. At least slightly flawed."

Eliza stared at him and blinked. The idea that someone might think she was anywhere near perfect was so strange that she was stunned into silence. Or was he mocking her?

"Perfect? Are you making fun of me?"

Michael frowned, "No. You asked me that once before. I've never met a woman who accepted compliments with less grace than you. Or deserved them more."

"I can accept compliments. When they're not so . . . unbelievable and exaggerated."

"Exaggerated? Unbelievable? You don't see yourself the way I do." Michael came to stand before her. He traced the curve of her cheek with his index finger. "The way the light strikes your skin, and your skin absorbs and reflects it—it's as close to being luminous as human skin can get. That's perfect."

"Genes. Hendrika's legacy," Eliza shrugged.

"Hendrika?"

"My grandmother."

His hand lifted her hair and it slid through his fingers like silk. "Your hair. Its color and texture. A painter's dream."

"Good nutrition," she said.

He let his thumbs rest on her cheekbones. "Great bone structure."

"Heredity. My mother's side of the family."

"Perfect teeth."

"Expensive orthodontia."

"And no matter what you wear, you always look self-assured, composed, and poised." *And sexy,* though Michael didn't say that out loud.

Eliza opened her mouth and shut it. She could not think of a flip comeback to save her life. Even worse, she felt a blush creep into her face. Quickly, lightly, she said, "Where's my mother when someone says something nice about me?" *Except Gloria would take one look at Michael's ponytail and tell me to consider the source.*

"Mom doesn't always approve of you?"

That was putting it mildly. "Let's just say that I'm not the daughter she dreamed of having."

"She'd have preferred one who liked shopping?"

". . . and long lunches, discussing the pros and cons of a particular designer while feasting on arugula leaves and sipping Perrier . . . Or one who had a suitable job, was planning a fancy wedding—"

"You don't want to get married?"

"I do, but I don't want a wedding that takes the greater part of a year to plan. I'd just as soon elope."

"You would?"

"Yes. You obviously haven't been to the kind of wedding I'm talking about. I have been to many and I've been a bridesmaid a few times. You know the worst part about big weddings?"

Michael shook his head.

"Somehow the vows and the two people pledging them seem to get lost in the spectacle of the occasion. The most important part is shortchanged." Eliza could not interpret the expression in Michael's midnight-black eyes. Had she revealed too much? Would he guess the truth about her background? She flicked another look at him. He had not, but she needed to be more careful. Quickly she cast about for a different topic.

"I can stay another hour. You want to continue?" she asked.

"I'm game, but are you sure you can do it?"

"I am."

"Are your shoulders still stiff?"

Eliza lifted them up toward her ears, held the pose and then released the stretch. "A little," she admitted.

Michael's hands grasped her shoulders. "Let me work on these muscles."

Before Eliza could protest that the time would be better spent painting, his fingers skillfully manipulated her sore muscles. It felt so good that all thoughts of stopping him vanished.

"Better? Does it feel good?"

He had no idea. "Yes," Eliza murmured, closing her eyes. She placed her hands on his chest to steady herself. The odor of paint and turpentine clinging to him, the smell of his soap, and the innate scent that branded him as Michael, filled her senses. She felt a sweet lethargy flow through her veins like fine cognac. No longer earthbound, she felt as if she and Michael were ensconced in their private universe—a universe consisting of scent and touch and emotion.

In her mind's eye they became like Chagall's lovers, floating serenely above the roofs of a dark city. *Lovers.* What a wonderful word. Full of magic and promise.

"What are you thinking about?" Michael asked.

"Chagall."

Michael pulled back a little farther to study her face. "Yeah? He's a favorite of mine, but he doesn't make me smile such a dreamy smile. Is the smell of turpentine making you lightheaded?" he asked, seemingly concerned.

She shook her head. Eliza felt definitely and deliciously light-headed, but not because of the turpentine. Most women would probably wrinkle their noses at the smell, but to Eliza it was purely enchanting . . . exhilarating . . . aphrodisiacal.

Aphrodisiacal? Since when did the scent of a studio affect her so potently? Of course, she knew the answer instantly. Only with Michael did paint and turpentine equal sensuous bliss. Only with him did this scent not only awaken, but overload each of her senses. This could be dangerous. What if it prevented her from posing properly for Michael? What if it wasted his time, or kept him from painting? Under no circumstances could Eliza allow this to happen.

She took two steps back. "I'm ready to pose again," she said and took her position behind the table. She picked up the phlox and pretended to add it to the flowers already in the blue vase. Her shoulder muscles protested. Ignoring them, she said, "You know these flowers will wilt before the painting is finished."

"That's why I'm painting them first. I also photographed them, just in case," Michael said as he approached Eliza.

For a moment she thought she might be off the mark,

but glancing at her feet, she saw that she was standing right behind the chalk mark on the floor. "What's wrong?"

"Just a few minor adjustments." Michael pulled the sleeves of her peasant blouse a little farther down her arms. "I want to see and paint as much of your luminous skin as I can." He traced the bare slopes of her shoulders toward her neck.

Her skin felt like satin under his fingertips—like warm, perfumed satin. The color of satin was warm white. *Warm. Warmhearted.* These were some of the adjectives he associated with Eliza. What he knew about her background, and admittedly it was not much, suggested that she ought to be cool, reserved and stand-offish. But she was far from it. Michael knew how passionate she was about art. He strongly suspected that if she let herself go, she would be as passionate physically. The thought almost buckled his knees.

"Does touching a subject make it easier to paint?" Eliza asked, raising her face to look at him.

"Yes . . . no," Michael shrugged. "I don't know for sure, but I think it does," he admitted. He had never consciously thought about it before, but suddenly realized it might be true—though not of all subjects he had painted or would paint. He had not felt the slightest inclination to touch any of the cowboys in the rodeo paintings, or the fancy dancers in their bright costumes at the powwow. But he sure wanted and needed to touch Eliza. Michael leaned closer, his lips almost touching her shoulder.

She felt his breath like a feather against her skin. The

sensation was a little like being tickled and a whole lot like being caressed. Was Michael going to kiss her shoulder, her neck? Eliza stood still, not daring to move and let the sensuous moment pass. Finally, not being able to endure the suspense any longer, she whispered, "Michael, what are you doing?"

"Trying to identify your fragrance. It clings to your skin and your hair. Don't women usually dab perfume just behind the ears?"

"It's not perfume."

"No?"

"It's a scented oil that a woman in Paris mixed for me. I put a few drops into my bath water and into a fragrance-free shampoo. Do you like it?" she asked a little breathlessly.

"Oh yeah, it's a lovely, mysterious green scent."

"Green?"

"Scents have color. I just can't figure out the components. Usually I can recognize at least one flower in a perfume."

"It's geranium. The woman said the main floral ingredient was geranium—that's a flowering plant people usually keep on their window sills. It's mixed with a little bit of jasmine and sandalwood. Simone also said she added herbs and spices like sage and citron and other stuff I can't remember."

Why was she going on and on about the blasted ingredients? Probably to keep from swooning. Eliza could not accurately define or describe swooning, but she had a strong feeling that she might find out quickly and personally what swooning was. Unless she grabbed

Michael and kissed him to end this sweet, suspenseful torture.

The light, tantalizing touch of his fingertips on her skin and his nearness made her tremble. Michael must have felt her response. His hands gripped her shoulders firmly and molded her against him. Eliza was sure he was going to kiss her, but after looking at her for a long, smoldering moment, he released her abruptly and walked to the window.

With his back to her, he said, "We'd better call it a day."

"But I thought we'd work for another hour or so."

Michael made a show of clenching and unclenching his right hand.

"Oh, of course. You're tired. I didn't realize your hand was fatigued."

His hand was not fatigued, and he was not tired, but he had made the mistake of touching Eliza. As long as he kept his distance and only looked at her as the subject of his painting, he was okay. But heaven help him if he touched her. It brought him dangerously close to abandoning all the dreams, plans, and goals he had pursued for the past ten years.

"We'll continue tomorrow morning," he said, his voice as gruff as he could make it. He had to keep Eliza at arm's length. He had to protect himself against the powerful magnetism she emitted—magnetism he could easily succumb to unless he was unblinkingly on guard.

Eliza, puzzled by his tone, waited a moment. When he did not say anything else, she said, "All right," and stepped behind the screen to change her clothes.

"You know, when you said you'd provide clothes for me to wear, I thought you'd bring one of the tie-dye T-shirts you talked about."

"I'm surprised you remembered that."

If pressed, Eliza could probably quote everything Michael had ever said to her, though she would certainly not admit that to him.

"The T-shirt wasn't right for the mood I wanted," he explained.

Gently Eliza touched the delicate white-on-white embroidery on the blouse Michael had bought for her before she placed it on a hanger. She stepped out from behind the screen and picked up her shoulder bag.

"On Sunday I'm having a few people over to my place—sort of a housewarming. Will you come? After all, you helped paint the apartment." When he did not answer right away, she added, "There'll be a buffet brunch."

"That cinches it," he said with the smallest of smiles. "Offer a bachelor a home-cooked meal and he's putty in your hands."

If only that were true. "Good. I've also invited John and Winona," Eliza said.

"She may have the baby between now and then," Michael warned. "She's past her due date."

"I know, but Gran says that babies have no regard for due dates or calendars. Anyway, come around ten."

Eliza looked at her sideboard critically. She thought it looked all right, but then she had never set up a buffet table before. She had never even fixed a meal for more than two people. And that she had done only twice, both times for Michael.

Michael had been serious, solemn, and reserved all week. It seemed to her that he had deliberately kept his distance. He had not touched her once, not even to adjust her hair or her sleeves. Had she hurt his feelings? Eliza went over every conversation, every nuance, every gesture, again and again but could not come up with anything that could be construed as hurtful or insulting. So why was he so aloof? She had no clue.

With a sigh she turned to the table she had set with a pretty linen cloth. She moved the potted geranium a little to the left. The red flowers and deep green leaves made a simple but lovely centerpiece. She hoped her guests would be pleased. Guests? There was one guest she especially wanted to please and impress—Michael.

The doorbell rang. Perhaps he had come early. Eliza moved quickly, eagerly, to the door and opened it. When she saw her grandmother and Sturges, she tried bravely to suppress the disappointment she felt. She hugged Hendrika and smiled at Sturges who handed her a wrapped package. Eliza invited them in with a gesture.

"What's this? Gran, I said no presents. Or is it something you asked your cook to fix? Don't you trust me to prepare a simple meal?"

"Darling, I trust you implicitly. You can do anything you set your mind to doing. It isn't food," Hendrika said. "It's something I made for you."

Eliza squeezed the package.

"Go on and open it," Hendrika said with a smile.

Eliza tore the wrapping paper and removed the small

needlepoint pillow. "How lovely." She placed the pillow on the couch and stepped back to admire it. "Perfect . . . Very van Gogh."

"I'm glad you like it. When you told me that you'd bought blue slipcovers for your sofa, I thought the sunflower pillow would complement it."

"It does." Eliza flashed her grandmother a smile before hurrying to the door. Whoever had rung the doorbell, had done so insistently, the way her mother always did. She opened the door and was not surprised.

"Mom, I thought it would be you, since you're the only one I know who keeps her finger on the bell for a good seven seconds."

"Cuts down on the time I have to wait outside." Gloria came in, greeted Hendrika, nodded to Sturges, and handed Eliza an envelope. "Go on. Open it."

Eliza did. It contained a generous check. "Mom, this wasn't necessary."

Gloria waved her hand dismissingly. "Use it to buy what you need for this place." She inspected the living room. "Not bad," she conceded. "You do have an eye for color and form. I'll give you that. Too bad you didn't pick a better neighborhood."

"I couldn't afford one," Eliza said.

Gloria snorted daintily. "If you'd asked him, your father would buy you a lakefront condo with a doorman on duty to keep the undesirables out."

Eliza calculated that she could probably buy one for herself but didn't say so. "Mom, I'm too old to ask my father to buy me things. I want to earn them. Besides, I don't want a lakefront condo. At least not now."

Gloria raised an eyebrow. "Which means that you're still interested in that painter. The one from whom you've kept the truth about your social and financial standing."

"I invited Michael. You won't give me away, will you?" Eliza asked, her voice edged with pleading.

Gloria looked at her daughter for a long moment and sighed, "I won't, but not for the reasons you probably think."

Eliza wondered what agenda her mother had—and she almost always had one—but before she could ask, Gloria spoke again.

"He's not a bad artist, judging by the two paintings Charles bought. By the way, your stepfather sends his apologies. He had to meet some important clients for a round of golf." Gloria allowed herself a small, deprecating smile. "Men and their games!"

"Not all men play games," Eliza said, but her tone lacked conviction.

"Oh, yes, they do. It may not be golf, but they all play games. Competitive games, manipulative games, mind games."

Did Michael play games? Uneasily Eliza wondered if his cool-hot attitude toward her was a game. If it was, what did he hope to gain? Was he trying to keep her off balance? If that's what he wanted, he had certainly succeeded. But why would he want to keep her guessing about his feelings for her? If he did not care about her, she could accept that. But if he did care, why pretend sometimes otherwise?

Was he being coy? Eliza dismissed that adjective

immediately. It seemed to her that coyness was prima-
rily a feminine trait. Possibly because of that poem she
remembered something from English class about a coy
mistress and there not being time enough to waste on
teasing games.

If she were more aggressive, she would demand an
explanation for his attitude, but she was not.
Confrontations were something she abhorred and
avoided. The ringing of the doorbell roused her from
her worrisome thoughts. Quickly, she opened the door.

"Winona!" Eliza exclaimed with a smile. "I'm so
glad you could make it, though I suspect you'd rather
be in the maternity ward about now."

"No offense, Eliza, but I sure would. This pregnancy
seems to go on and on." She handed Eliza a basket
lined with a cloth napkin.

Eliza sniffed. "Did you make fry bread? You
shouldn't have. Aren't you supposed to be resting with
your feet up?"

"That gets old fast," Winona said with a grimace.

"Trying to get her to rest is worse than wrestling a
grizzly for honey," John said, which earned him a mild
slap on the arm and a loving smile from his wife.

Hendrika came forward to be introduced. The for-
malities completed, Eliza said, "Gran, wait 'til you
taste this fry bread. I don't know exactly what manna
from heaven is, but this has to come close."

"I look forward to having a piece," Hendrika said.
"Winona, come and sit in this straight-backed chair. I
remember when I was pregnant how hard it was to get
up out of a so-called comfortable chair."

Eliza was about to shut the door, when Michael appeared.

"Am I late? I was painting and lost track of time."

"You're not late." Even if he were, it would not have mattered. He had come and that was enough to make her giddy with joy. Remembering that she was the hostess she said, "Come on in and meet everyone."

Eliza watched her grandmother's expression when she introduced Michael. Hendrika smiled at him. Her mother did not, but her voice was not unfriendly. Thank heaven for small favors.

While her guests served themselves, Michael joined Eliza in the kitchen.

"I brought you a housewarming present." He handed her a small, square package wrapped in white tissue paper.

"I know everybody says, 'you shouldn't have,' but I meant it when I said so the other day." Eliza ran her finger over the package. Something hard. Framed? With mounting excitement she ripped the paper off. Her breath caught in her throat. She was not sure if she would ever breathe normally again.

"Don't you like it? I remembered you talking about the scent of geraniums, so I thought you might like a painting of the flowers—"

"Oh, it's beautiful," Eliza whispered, obviously overwhelmed. "You managed to capture the shade of my favorite geranium. Red with just a touch of orange. It's the most beautiful flower painting I've ever seen." Eliza threw her arms around Michael and hugged him. "Thank you."

"You're welcome," he murmured, his voice husky and pleased.

"It's amazing that we both chose the same geranium. Did you look at the plant on my buffet?"

"I saw it when I came in, and you could have knocked me over with a feather. I mean, what are the odds that both of us would pick the same color?"

Eliza shrugged with a smile. "Maybe not likely, but certainly not impossible." Their tastes ran along similar lines. Every day Eliza discovered something new that they had in common. She ached to hug him again.

"Where do you think you will hang it? It isn't very large."

"It's absolutely perfect, and I know exactly where it'll go." She had had to hang the still life at her grandmother's house but this one would stay in the apartment. "I'll hang it between the two windows in my bedroom. I'll see it first thing when I wake up every day," she said softly. *See it and think of you. Long for you.*

Their eyes met and held for several seconds. Then Michael's gaze dropped to her mouth. Eliza's toes curled. He was kissing her without touching her.

A genteel throat-clearing broke the spell.

"Eliza, is there some water?" Gloria asked. "Winona would like some."

"Yes, there's a pitcher in the refrigerator. Look at the watercolor Michael gave me."

Gloria studied the small painting. "It's absolutely lovely," she said.

From her mother's tone Eliza could tell that Gloria meant it. Chalk up a plus for Michael. Eliza practically danced to the refrigerator to fetch the water pitcher which she carried into the living room.

After she poured a glass of water for Winona, Eliza took Michael's hand and led him to her grandmother. She handed the painting to Hendrika. "Michael painted this for me. Isn't it beautiful?"

"Oh my. It certainly is." Hendrika looked at Michael. "Eliza said you were good, but I had no idea you were this talented. She also said you're getting ready for a one-man show. When will that be?"

"Early in December," Michael said and crossed his fingers.

"I'm partial to flowers. Any chance of a watercolor similar to this one being in the show?"

"I've already painted a still life with pink phlox. The same phlox that's in Eliza's portrait."

"You're painting my daughter?" Gloria asked, her brows drawn into a frown.

"Relax, Mom. It's not a nude."

"I should hope not! I'd hate to have half of Chicago staring at my daughter's nude body."

Eliza rolled her eyes. "Michael, let's get something to eat." She steered him toward the buffet.

As soon as they were out of earshot, Gloria said to Hendrika, her voice low, accusing, furious, "I can't believe you let this go so far. Eliza is obviously infatuated with that young man. Maybe even in love. How could you?"

Hendrika fixed her ex-daughter-in-law with a stern look. "What could I have done? Forbid Eliza to see Michael? Pack her off to Europe? She's no longer a teenager, but an independent young woman with a mind of her own. There's nothing I—or you—can do."

"We'll see about that."

"Besides, there's nothing wrong with Michael. I had the detective agency check him out. He's talented and hard working. He seems like a decent young man. And he's not at all like—"

"Don't say it! You promised never to talk about it," Gloria said, her voice low, anxious. Pulling herself together, she added, "He's hardly our kind. He and Eliza have about as much in common as—"

"Don't be such a snob and don't interfere," Hendrika warned.

"How can I not interfere when my daughter is about to make the biggest mistake of her life?"

"Are you so sure it's a mistake? Eliza has a good head on her shoulders. I trust her to make the right decision."

"Well, I'm not that trusting," Gloria snapped.

"Are you going to tell Michael the truth?"

"No, I won't have to."

"What are you up to?" Hendrika asked, a feeling of unease gripping her.

Gloria shrugged, her expression enigmatic.

Chapter Seven

Eliza looked around the apartment. Everything had been put away after the brunch, the dishes washed, the leftovers stored. In the stillness of the afternoon she thought she heard echoes of the laughter and conversation. Smiling, she shook her head at the notion.

Her first party had been a success! Even her mother had been pleasant to everyone including Michael, except at the end she had turned a little odd. Her mother, who prided herself on never showing strong emotions, had almost quivered with nervous energy, like a woman who had suddenly found a mission. Though Eliza had no idea what that mission might be, she had the unsettling suspicion that perhaps it ought to worry her.

Yawning, she dismissed her unease. She was tired and ready for bed. Even on her day off, Eliza had learned to stick to the schedule her graveyard shift demanded. She pulled the drapes, shutting out the sun. She jumped a little when the doorbell rang.

"Who on earth?" she muttered, opening the door as far as the safety chain allowed. When she saw who it was, her voice deserted her for several seconds.

"Rick? What are you doing here?" she asked finally. She had not expected him back in town so soon. Actually, she had forgotten all about him.

"Hello, Eliza. Are you going to let me in?"

For a moment she debated closing the door on him, but at some point she would have to face him. It might as well be now. With a sigh she unfastened the chain and motioned him in.

"Thanks for inviting me to your open house," he said.

He had not lost his talent for tinging his voice with just enough edge to suggest sarcasm. "I thought you were still out of town, checking on your company's plant in . . . Mexico? Thailand? Taiwan?"

"Mexico. I've been back for a couple of days but I expected you to be at the spa."

Eliza ignored both Rick's critical glare as well as his pointed reference to the fat farm. "How did you know about this apartment?"

"Your mo—what difference does it make how I know?"

"Mom." That explained Gloria's sudden change in temperament. She could hardly wait to contact Rick. She must have phoned him the moment she left the apartment.

"What are you doing in this place?" he demanded.

"Seems to me that's obvious. I live here."

He made a point of looking slowly around the darkened room. His lips curled down at the corners, showing Eliza exactly what he thought of her apartment.

"Why? Why would you willingly live in this second-hand, second-rate dump when you could be luxuriating at your grandmother's place, having Sturges take care of everything?"

The words "second-hand" and "second-rate" caused Eliza to clench her hands into fists. To resist the temptation to slug Rick, Eliza shoved her hands into the pockets of the apron Sturges had given her as a hostess present.

"And what's this?" Rick reached out to touch the apron.

Quickly, Eliza moved back, evading his hand.

"An apron? Eliza, have you lost your mind? You weren't born to wear an apron."

"I and I alone will decide what I was born to wear," she said quietly, firmly, imperially.

"Wrong. Your family and your background decided that. You're not one of the great unwashed. And what's with that job of yours?"

"Great unwashed? When did you become familiar with proletarian rhetoric?" Even in the darkened room she could tell he flushed. "Maybe in the sweatshops your company uses in Mexico?" She watched his body stiffen into a defensive mode.

"They're not sweatshops," he protested, his tone

self-righteous. "We give jobs to people who never had jobs before."

"Maybe so, but didn't the people here at home need these same jobs? What about those who became unemployed when you moved your company out of the U.S. to take advantage of cheap labor?"

"Eliza, since when do you care anything about business? Let me tell you about—"

She raised her hand to stop him. "I'm not in the mood to debate business ethics with you or listen to your rationalizations. Why are you here?" she wanted to know.

"You're asking me that after all we've meant to each other? What's wrong with you? I bet it's that Indian painter you've been hanging out with who is filling your head with—"

"What we meant to each other?" she repeated, her voice rising a full octave. "We've had a series of dates over the years, a barely lukewarm romance, if it can be called that, which was going nowhere fast—"

"Going nowhere? How can you say that? There's always been an understanding that we'd join the two families' fortunes and become a formidable force in financial circles."

Formidable force in financial circles? Hearing the alliteration, Eliza suppressed a smile. When she had first met Rick, he had fancied himself a poet. There was nothing wrong with aiming high. And she had thought she would be a painter. They had been young and idealistic. It was funny how life turned out. But this was no time to be introspective. She had to set Rick straight about their future—or lack of one.

"There was an understanding," he repeated stubbornly.

"An understanding between my mother and you perhaps, but never with me," Eliza said, her voice firm.

"What are you saying? I've counted on us joining—"

"Well, *don't* count on it." Then she shook her head, her expression bewildered. "Rick, do you really think that you and I could possibly be happy together?"

"What's not to be happy about? We're a good match, both socially and financially. We—"

"Stop. There is no match. You and I will never be a match." Eliza looked at Rick suspiciously. "You've never been so eager before. What happened? What's changed?"

"Nothing's changed—except your moving to this place and getting a job," he shrugged.

He did not meet her gaze. She sensed a wariness in him, an evasiveness. Rick hunched his left shoulder. She had learned over the years that this was a telltale sign indicating he was not telling her the whole truth. When he moved toward her, she stepped to the side, putting the armchair between them.

"Rick, I'm tired. It's past my bedtime—"

"It's one o'clock in the afternoon!"

"When you work the graveyard shift, this is bedtime." Eliza walked to the door with determined steps. She opened it.

"I can't believe this! You're asking me to leave?"

"Yes."

"Why you—"

"Careful. Your lovely manners are slipping. My mother would be so disappointed if that happened." She watched him make a determined effort to pull himself together.

"We'll talk again when you're not so tired. This isn't the end of it."

"Yes, it is. Good-bye, Rick." Eliza closed the door on him before he could say anything else, but she believed him when he said this was not the end of it. What Eliza did not understand was why.

Why had Rick suddenly become so interested in her? Was it because of Michael, another man in the picture? A lot of men might be challenged by competition for a woman, but not Rick. He was not passionate enough for that. Or maybe he was just too arrogant to be drawn into a primitive male contest over a female.

What was it then? Eliza mulled over her conversation with Rick. He had mentioned the word *financial* several times. Money and status were things Rick could get passionate about. Could his family's business be in trouble?

Without hesitation Eliza dialed her stepfather's number. "How was your golf game?" she asked when Charles picked up the phone. Eliza listened patiently to the highlights until Charles paused to take a breath.

"The reason I'm calling, Charles, is to ask you something. It's an important question." Eliza paused for a beat. "Have you heard anything about Carr Enterprises being in financial trouble?"

The silence following her question was long and total. "So they *are* having problems," she concluded.

"Well, you know their pharmaceutical division lost that lawsuit over one of their products. It cost them a bundle."

"And?" Eliza prompted, sensing that there was more.

"And there have been rumors of earnings falling below projections, and of production falling behind schedule . . . ," his voice trailed off.

"Just rumors, or is there something concrete?"

"Strong rumors from reliable sources. I would not advise investing in Carr Enterprises right now."

That, Eliza thought, *is as good as a definite yes.*

"You're not thinking of investing—"

"No, no," she assured him. "I was just wondering why Rick Carr was suddenly so anxious to merge our financial fortunes, as he put it."

"Eliza, I wouldn't recommend that either. Actually, I'd discourage it strongly."

She heard his sharply indrawn breath when he realized what he had said.

"You won't tell your mother I said that, will you?"

"I won't. And I'm not about to hitch my financial or personal star to Rick's." Eliza heard her mother's voice in the background.

"Good. Don't do anything I advised against," Charles said in a tone meant to suggest he was conferring with a client.

She heard her mother ask who it was. A second before Eliza could say good-bye, Gloria took the phone.

"Eliza, what happened?"

"Nothing, Mom. I had to ask Charles for some professional advice. I'm sorry I interrupted your afternoon. I'll let him get back to whatever you were doing."

"Not so fast. Did Rick come to see you?"

"Yes. Thanks for siccing him on me."

"What a vulgar expression. Rick is hardly some mangy dog."

No, more like a nervous, finicky purebred. Eliza said, "I have to get some sleep now."

"Wait. What did Rick say?"

"Talked a lot about joining our financial assets."

"He didn't come right out and propose?" Gloria asked.

"Not after I said I wasn't about to conjoin our stock portfolios, personal properties, and trust funds."

"Eliza! How could you?"

"It was easy." Eliza took a breath. She had to convince her mother once and for all. "Mom, I'm not going to marry Rick. You might as well get used to the idea. Now I really have to get some sleep. Talk to you later."

Eliza hung up before her mother could reply. After activating the answering machine, Eliza fell into bed, but sleep did not come until she focused on Michael. He had chatted with ease and at length with her grandmother. He had taken two servings of her food. Who would have thought that feeding a man could be so deeply satisfying? With a smile on her face she drifted into sleep.

A week later, John phoned the studio just as Michael ended their session. While he spoke with his friend and partner, Eliza changed her clothes.

"John wants us to come over. The web site is up."

"How exciting!"

"Do you have time?" he asked.

"Since we finished early, I do."

The way she put a slight emphasis on *early*, Michael felt compelled to explain. " 'Eliza with Phlox' is finished. Actually your portrait was finished yesterday. Today I completed the background. Would you like to take a look?"

"Would I? Of course I want to see the painting. I wasn't sure you'd let me see it." Eliza rushed toward the easel, but came to an abrupt stop a couple of feet from the painting. She was not sure she was ready to confront Michael's vision of her, given his ambivalent attitude toward her in the past days. Yet no power on earth could keep her from wanting to take a look.

"Having second thoughts?" he asked. "Afraid it won't be good?" His voice held a trace of disappointment, maybe even a little hurt.

Quickly she said, "I know it'll be good. I have no doubt about that. But it's a little scary to find out how someone else sees you. I don't mean that I expect you to have flattered me. I'd be disappointed if you had. But your painter's eyes may have perceived something that no one else has seen—maybe not even me." Eliza looked at him in silence, wanting him to understand what she meant.

He nodded and held out his hand to her.

This was the first time he had offered to touch her since she had spontaneously hugged him when he had given her the watercolor at brunch. Eliza placed her slightly trembling hand in his.

He pulled her toward the painting until she stood squarely in front of it. Michael stepped aside and slightly forward so that he could see her expression. He heard her slight intake of breath, saw the widening of her eyes and waited while she studied the painting with rapt concentration.

"Well?" he asked, unable to wait any longer.

"It's beautiful," she said simply, softly, "but surely you know that."

"I needed to hear you say it." He felt immense satisfaction and validation. "But there was an unspoken *but* at the end of your sentence. What is it?"

Eliza looked at him. "I didn't know I had sad eyes."

"You don't always. But sometimes when you're deep in thought, there's a sadness there. I've studied your eyes because they were a challenge to paint." Michael looked at her searchingly. "It's maybe not so much sadness as aloneness. Solitude."

He had not quite come out and said so, but was he labeling her with that most despicable of all epithets: poor little rich girl? Surely not. Michael did not know anything about her financial status.

"Being solitary isn't the worst way to be," she said defensively.

"No, it's not. As an artist I need and appreciate a certain amount of solitude."

She heard his unspoken question. "Since I'm not an artist, why am I—"

"Yes." Michael waited, wondering if she would tell him that this was a presumptuous question and none of his business. But seeing her day after day, he could not help but be intensely curious about her. Curious? Fascinated was more like it. Fortunately, he'd been able to look at her as his subject and thus had been able to refrain from touching her, at least with his hands. His eyes, however, had caressed every inch of her lovely face, her shoulders—

"I suppose I *was* a solitary child," Eliza mused. "When my parents divorced, my dad took Peter and my mom took me. She's not a woman who manages well on her own. Charles is her fourth husband, so there have been lots of changes, moves, and new people in my life. After her second divorce I guess I figured it didn't pay to get attached since everyone was bound to leave."

"Do you still think that?" Michael asked.

She shook her head. "It took a long time before I realized that it was a lot better to let people into your life, even if they ultimately left."

Eliza stopped speaking. Then she smiled, but it was a quivery, tentative smile. "I've never told this to anyone. You're a dangerous man, Michael Yuma."

"Not really. Just a good listener and observer."

"So people tell you things."

"Yes, but I would never betray a confidence or use it against anyone."

Eliza looked at him. She believed him.

"You had your grandmother. I like her. She's a terrific lady."

This time Eliza's smile was joyous. "Yes, she is.

Hendrika was always there for me. I swore to myself that I'd always be there for her, especially as she gets older."

She looked at the painting again. "It's good. Very good. I wonder who'll buy it."

"Maybe I'll just exhibit it, but not sell it."

"That wouldn't be smart," Eliza said firmly. "Your paintings need to be out there for people to see. Besides, I'm not sure the gallery would let you do that."

"You're probably right. And I have the original to look at," Michael said and turned her to face him.

"Yes, you do." *For as long as you like which I hope is forever,* Eliza added silently.

"Will you sit for another painting?"

Eliza's heart leaped. Since his hands rested on her shoulders, she was sure Michael had to feel her excitement. "Yes," she murmured.

"I'd hoped you'd say that. I have it all planned."

Eliza's hands slid around his waist. She leaned against him. He felt so good. She did not want to move, to let him go. They stood like that, holding each other for several heartbeats. Eliza thought she felt Michael's lips touching her hair.

"I suppose we better get to Sun Designs or you'll not get enough sleep before you have to go to work."

With a suppressed sigh, Eliza unwound her arms.

Michael was acutely aware of Eliza as he sat next to her before the computer screen. He liked sitting this close to her—close enough to breathe in the scent of geranium, a flower that had become a favorite. It was true that the loveliness of the geranium did not rival the showy beauty of a rose, but its petals were perfectly symmetrical, the edges of the leaves precisely scalloped, and as a whole, a study in quiet harmony, charm, and appeal. Like Eliza herself.

Michael could not deny that he had liked it when she had put her arms around him and leaned against him. He had liked that she had trusted him enough to confide in him. Was there anything about this woman he did not like? He did not think so, and that was the trouble—or was it?

Eliza had shown none of the possessive and selfish qualities that would interfere with his painting. Actually, she was a bit of a slave driver when it came to his work. So why was he still fighting his attraction to her?

Was he still distrustful of a serious relationship because of his disastrous involvement with the woman who wanted him to give up painting and get a real job? She had been jealous of the time he spent in front of an easel, and hated his paintings.

Ultimately he had had to choose between love and art. The choice had not been easy or painless, but it had been inevitable. Even as young as he had been, he had known not to forsake his God-given talent.

Eliza's animated voice brought Michael's attention back to the computer.

"The web site is good. I like how quickly you can go from one screen to the next. The colors are great."

"Thanks," John said, who stood behind them, looking at the screen over their shoulders.

"But?" Michael asked, having caught Eliza's slight hesitation.

"Just a small suggestion," she said, her voice apologetic. "I like how you can get a detailed view of the front of the garment, but I'd like it even better if I could see a close-up of the back."

"That's going to run into money," John said.

"You wouldn't need a back view of every item. Just the ones that feature an interesting detail, like that black pencil skirt I modeled. It's a classic, but what moves it up a notch is the row of small buttons along the kick pleat. Then there are those dresses that have ties in the back to allow the waist to be adjusted. And remember the linen tunic that has that half-belt in back with—"

"Yeah, and the jackets with the embroidery on the back," John said, catching Eliza's enthusiasm.

She nodded, "Those are all selling features. I think they need to be emphasized."

"You're right. Except we're just about out of money," John said. He paced a few steps, his expression worried.

"Then get a small business loan."

John and Michael exchanged a look.

"What?" Eliza asked.

"You make it sound so easy. Two guys off the rez, marching into a bank, asking for a loan . . . ," John shook his head.

"The two guys off the rez are also talented and smart and have a product that has a great chance to succeed if marketed properly." Eliza took a notebook, a pen, and a business card from her shoulder bag. Quickly she wrote several lines on it.

"Remember, I told you about my brother, Peter, who specializes in loans to small businesses? Here's his card. And here are the points you have to stress when you apply for a loan. I know this because I've heard him talk about them often enough."

Michael watched Eliza, fascinated. How decisive she was, and how confident. What kind of upbringing did it take to develop that kind of confidence? Their backgrounds seemed to be one crucial point of difference between them. Was it something they could overcome? Realizing where his thoughts were heading, he called himself a fool and a dreamer.

Why was he speculating about their compatibility? Nothing had happened between them. Eliza liked his work, but did she like him? Enough to be serious? Or was she slumming? *No, she's not like that,* he told himself. *She's different. Genuine.* At least he liked to think so.

"Give Peter a call today," Eliza urged. She glanced at her watch. "He's probably out to lunch right now, but in an hour he should be back in his office." She rose.

"I have to go or I'll be a zombie at work tonight." Eliza said a quick good-bye and hurried out.

She needed to speak to Peter before John called for an appointment. She had no doubt that they would receive the loan, but she wanted to be sure that the process was quick and without a hassle.

Peter usually went to lunch at a deli near the bank. Eliza drove there. For once, traffic was not a nightmare. She even found a nearby parking space.

Eliza saw him as soon as she entered the deli. He was alone, eating a sandwich while reading the newspaper spread out on the table beside him. She slid into the chair opposite him.

"Eliza? What a surprise." His smile faltered. "What's wrong?" he demanded.

"Nothing. Why should something be wrong?"

"Because you don't often join me for lunch and when you do, there's usually a problem."

"It's not a problem exactly."

"Let's talk about it after I get you some food." Peter motioned to the waitress. "What'll you have?"

"A spinach salad and iced tea," she said without consulting the menu, eager to get to the topic of her visit.

"So, tell me about this thing that isn't a problem exactly," Peter said with a smile.

"There are these two guys, John Otterman and Michael Yuma who're going to ask you for a loan. They—"

"Michael Yuma? Isn't he the painter of those two landscapes Charles bought?"

"Yes, that's Michael."

"I liked the paintings."

Eliza smiled. "He's a very good artist. Anyway, they have this business they're trying to get off the ground." Eliza stopped to gather her thoughts. Then she presented her case. When she finished, she looked expectantly at her brother.

"So, you want me to give them a small business loan?"

"Yes. They've never applied for a loan, so I don't know how well they'll present their case, but if you have any doubt, I'll guarantee the loan. Put up collateral. You know I'm good for it."

Peter raised an eyebrow. "You'll do that for them? For him? Michael?"

"Yes, but you can't tell him." Eliza pressed Peter's arm for emphasis. "Promise you won't."

"All right, all right. I promise." Peter studied his sister's face. "You're in love with Michael."

It wasn't a question, but a flat statement. "Maybe." Eliza shrugged.

"I don't think there's a maybe about it, Sis. How does he feel about you?"

"I'm not sure. He's concentrating on painting. He's got a one-man show coming up and nothing can distract him from getting ready for it. I understand that. He ignores me as a woman. I understand why he has to do that, too."

"I shouldn't think it would be easy to ignore you."

"Oh, I hope not," Eliza said fervently. She took her cell phone from her bag and held it out to Peter. "Please call your secretary and tell her to give them an appointment as soon as possible. Tomorrow afternoon? Please? They're going to call after lunch."

Peter sighed, "You can be pushy and persuasive when you believe in something—or someone."

* * *

At her apartment door, Eliza saw one of those long boxes used by florists. For a heart-stopping second she wondered if Michael had sent her flowers. Not likely. Money was tight. Besides, he would probably sketch a bouquet for her, which would be infinitely better because it would last forever.

She took the box inside. When she read the card, she grimaced. *Rick.* She dumped the box in the trash can. "Way too late," she muttered, "thank heaven." She opened the window by the fire escape. A few seconds later, the gray-and-white cat appeared.

"Hi, there, handsome. I'll get your food." Before Eliza was halfway to the kitchen, she sensed the cat behind her. She continued to the kitchen. Unhurried, so as not to alarm him, she filled his bowl with water and set it on the floor. She heard him lap the water eagerly while she poured cat food into a dish. He sat, his tail curled around him, waiting in patient dignity.

Eliza took a bottle of water from the fridge and drank it while she watched him. As he ate, his amber eyes darted an occasional watchful look at her. "I'm so glad you came in. You are welcome to live with me."

The cat ignored her invitation and when he finished eating, proceeded to wash his face with precise, unhurried movements similar to those Michael used when painting.

Michael. What was he doing now? Probably standing in front of his easel, painting. Her brother's question haunted her. How *did* Michael feel about her? She thought he was attracted to her when he allowed himself to be. She had to wait until after his show to find out for sure. It would not be fair to distract him now.

Two months seemed like a long time, but Eliza possessed great patience when something was worth waiting for. And Michael was.

Chapter Eight

When Eliza left the shelter two days later, she felt uneasy. She kept checking the rearview mirror, looking for the white van she thought had been following her the day before. This morning she did not spot it, but every time she looked, a green pickup was right behind her. In the front seat were two men wearing baseball caps. Just as there had been in the van.

Eliza shook her head. She would hate to have to count the number of vehicles containing two men sharing a ride to work on any given morning. She told herself she was getting alarmed over nothing.

When she turned into Michael's street, so did the pickup. Eliza parked and the pickup drove past her. With her cell phone in hand, she sat in her truck for five minutes, waiting to see if the pickup would park nearby or pass again. It did neither. Relieved, Eliza got out of her truck.

Michael met her at the door. "Why were you sitting in your truck? Is something wrong?"

Embarrassed, Eliza shrugged. "I thought a green pickup was following me, but apparently I was wrong."

Michael stepped out into the street looking up and down but saw nothing out of the ordinary. "You want to report this to the cops?" he asked, following Eliza into the studio.

"What's to report? I'm not even sure I *was* followed." Eliza looked around. "I see you've got the camera set up. What am I wearing?"

Michael picked up a box with the logo of a well-known department store on it. He handed it to her. "This . . . if you don't mind."

Eliza looked at the lacy garment, her eyes wide. "A slip?"

"The painting is tentatively titled, 'Eliza brushing her hair.' Sitting at that white dressing table," he said, pointing. "Do you mind posing in the slip?"

"No, but why a slip? Women brush their hair when they're fully dressed, too."

"True, but from a painter's point of view, skin is a lot more interesting than cloth. I want to paint your skin. Put the slip on, please. It's not too low-cut. I asked the sales lady for something pretty but modest."

Eliza changed into the slip behind the screen. It fit perfectly. She ran her hand over the smooth silver-gray satin. The lace on the bodice was exquisite. "How did you know what size to get? Have you bought slips for a lot of women?" she asked, still behind the screen.

"No, this is my first. Don't forget that even though I

wasn't interested in designing clothes the way John was, I couldn't escape learning a few things while he and my mother did alterations on women's garments."

"I'll bet you even know how to sew on a button."

"I do. It's come in handy a few times. Do you—"

Michael's voice broke off when Eliza stepped from behind the screen. He stared at her silently for so long that Eliza became self-conscious. "It doesn't look right?"

"No, it looks great. Even better than I envisioned. The lace will form an interesting pattern of shadows. Come and sit at the dressing table."

Eliza did. Michael asked her to brush her hair. He moved the lights and then took some photos. He stopped and looked at her.

"No, that's not right." He moved the dressing table out of the way. He took the brush from her hand and gently brushed her hair. He had meant to brush only a few strokes but now he did not seem to be able to stop. Who would have thought that brushing a woman's hair could be such a sensual experience? And this was not just any woman's hair, it was Eliza's. He felt the pleasure of touching the silky strands skitter all the way up his arms.

"This feels so good," Eliza murmured.

He stopped and looked at her accusingly. "Why do I always forget that I can't touch you?" He said his thoughts aloud this time.

"I'm not stopping you, so why can't you?"

"Because once I start I might not be able to stop. I would forget about painting and . . ."

"I wouldn't let you forget. Trust me."

Michael looked at her for a long moment. Then, without a word, he drew her to her feet. In a swift motion he wrapped his arms around her and kissed her. He had kissed her before, but this time it was different, more fiery, more hungry, more urgent. Eliza abandoned herself to his kiss and willed it to go on forever. But she had made a promise. Reluctantly she pulled away.

Picking up the brush, she asked, "How do you want me to pose?"

Silently he rearranged the lights and photographed her in half a dozen different poses, using no more than half a dozen words of instruction. None of the poses seemed to please him. While the kiss had left Eliza feeling gloriously alive and happy, it had left Michael silent, even a little grumpy. Men were so opaque. Like a dab of murky Prussian blue on a palette. He had asked her to stop him and when she had, he seemed resentful. Eliza repressed a sigh.

And then there was Rick, who had sent flowers daily, phoned her with invitations until she had simply stopped answering her phone. There would have to be another confrontation. This time Eliza would be brutally frank with Rick. Hopefully he would get the message. Men. Who understood them? She repressed another sigh.

"I'm glad I let my hair grow all summer," she said to break the silence. "Doesn't long hair look better in the sort of portrait you want?"

Eliza lowered her left arm, causing the strap of the slip to slide down her arm.

"Leave it down," Michael said and took a series of photos. Finally, he seemed to have found a pose that inspired him.

"Is something going on between them?" Rick demanded. "You've been following her for three days now."

The older man, Big Bob, shuffled from one foot to the other but said nothing. The shorter man, Jocko, answered, "It's hard to tell. We don't follow her inside the painter's place."

Rick swore. "His place has windows . . . *big* windows. It's an artist's studio."

"The windows in front have blinds that are always shut," Jocko said.

"He's a painter, guys. He has to have light. Hasn't it occurred to you birdbrains to look for windows in the back?"

"You mean go to the back through the alley?" Big Bob asked, alarmed.

"And why not?"

"There's always dogs in them alleys."

Rick looked toward the sky. "What led me to think the two of you had half a brain between you?" Rick glowered at the men with that superior look that reduced most people to a heap of anxiety and insecurity. "Listen to me. Tomorrow you'll follow her truck to his place. You'll park down the street and then you'll go to the alley. From there you'll find a spot to look through the window and observe what they're doing."

"What if he sees us?" Jocko asked.

"Duck behind a dumpster or something and he *won't* see you."

"That's a good idea," Big Bob said.

Rick gritted his teeth to keep from commenting further on the men's mental abilities. What had made him hire them? Then he remembered. The bartender at his favorite watering hole had recommended them as "willing to do anything for minimum pay." Rick reflected that you get what you pay for, even in thugs. If it were not so important to know what Eliza was up to with that painter, he would dismiss them on the spot. He drew a calming breath.

"What is it that you're going to do tomorrow?" he asked with the forced patience of a teacher five minutes before the dismissal bell.

"Follow the woman," Big Bob said, pleased with his answer.

"Sneak up behind the house and spy on them," Jocko added.

Rick did not like the word *spy*. It made him feel as if he were involved in some tawdry affair, and tawdry affairs were not his style. He adjusted his shirt cuffs until the requisite inch of fine, white linen extended beyond his jacket sleeves.

"Try not to be seen. It would be unfortunate if one of the neighbors called the police and had you picked up as Peeping Toms."

Big Bob's mouth dropped open at this possibility. Jocko looked as if he wanted to speak but Rick stopped him.

"Meet me tomorrow here at the park, after she leaves, to report. She usually goes home between noon and one?"

Jocko nodded.

"I'll see you then."

"How about our money?" Jocko asked.

"You'll get it tomorrow." Rick left them and quickly made his way through the crowd of senior citizens and moms with kids congregated in the park.

"You notice he ain't never told us his name?" Jocko said. "We don't know nothin' about him."

Big Bob looked at his friend, his expression bewildered.

"Don't it strike you funny? It's like he don't want us to know who he is."

"Yeah. And he don't talk nice to us."

"I think tomorrow we'll follow him and see what kind of car he drives."

"I know," Big Bob said, his voice excited. "I saw him pull into the parking lot the other day. He drives one of them fancy foreign cars. One of them sports cars."

"Are you sure?"

"I ain't as smart as you, Jocko, but I know cars."

"Yes, you do." Jocko thought for a moment. "You know what? We need to find out who the woman is."

"Yeah?"

"Yeah. Why is this dude so interested in her?"

"I guess he likes her and she's spendin' time with the painter."

Jocko nodded, tapping his nose. "Something don't

smell right about this. We'll follow the woman from the painter's place and see where she goes."

"If you say so, Jocko."

"Now, let's go and get a hot dog. That's about all we can afford until he pays us tomorrow."

The next day the two men hurried to the park a little late.

Rick was waiting for them. He looked pointedly at his watch. "Report," he snapped.

"We done like you told us. Snuck up to the window and watched," Jocko said. "He paints her."

Rick could feel his chest constrict. Had these two lowlifes seen Eliza without her clothes on? He found the thought of his future wife posing nude unendurable.

"What was she wearing?" he forced himself to ask.

"A slip," Jocko said.

Rick felt blood rush to his head. For a second he actually saw red. "A slip?"

"Yeah, you know . . . one of them lacy things women wear under their dresses."

These lowlifes had actually seen Eliza in a scanty undergarment. Rick vowed that she would pay dearly for this once she was his wife.

"She looked real pretty," Big Bob added which earned him a scathing look from Rick.

"What does she do?"

"She holds some flowers."

Rick breathed easier. *Holding flowers.* It could have been worse.

"And he fixes her hair and her slip strap," Jocko said,

having shrewdly guessed that Rick would not like that part of the report.

"They sorta like each other," Big Bob said with a grin.

Rick felt as if someone had punched him in the stomach. He took a moment to compose himself. So they liked each other. Wasn't that just too, too precious? He would soon put a stop to that. He knew he could not influence Eliza but how hard could it be to discourage and intimidate a struggling artist who did not have two dimes to rub together?

"Here is what I want you to do," Rick said. In the simplest of words he gave them exact instructions.

Eliza poured herself another cup of coffee, trying to get revved up for work. Glancing at the clock, she saw that she had two hours before she had to report for the graveyard shift.

The ring of the doorbell caused her hand to jerk, spilling coffee into the saucer. She was jumpy. On her way home from Michael's studio she thought she had seen the green pickup again. If only she could be sure—

The doorbell shrilled again. Eliza walked to the door. With her hand on the chain, she paused. What if it was Rick? She had told him flat out that she was not going to marry him. He had not liked it. Actually, she had the sinking feeling that he had not believed her, that he would continue to harass and bully her.

"Eliza?"

It was Michael's voice. She could not get the door open fast enough. "Hi. Sorry to keep you standing in the hall, but I thought it might be someone else."

"Who?" Michael asked with a frown.

"Rick." She made a dismissing gesture. "Nobody important. What brings you to my door?"

"Winona had her baby. A girl."

"How wonderful!"

"That's why I came by. You want to come with me? I—" He broke off when he saw the cat. "I told you he'd move in with you."

Eliza smiled. "Yes, you did. Handsome has made himself at home."

"Handsome? The name suits him."

As it suits you. In clean jeans and a neatly tucked-in chambray shirt, Michael looked incredibly good to her. The shirt looked and smelled freshly ironed. Had he learned to iron while watching his mother? Eliza loved the fact that he cared enough to iron his shirt.

Michael studied the big tomcat with interest. "He's just what I need in your portrait. I've tried adding a stack of books and a grouping of different-sized candles, but he'll be perfect. Do you mind if I photograph him?"

"You'd better if you want to use him. I doubt that you could persuade him to sit for you. Handsome does only what he wants to do."

"How nice for him," Michael said wistfully. "Most of us don't have that luxury. I'll get the camera from my car."

As soon as Michael was out the door, Eliza ran to the bathroom where she inspected her appearance. She did not look as bad as she had feared. Her hair was almost dry and ready to be curled. She plugged in the curling iron.

By the time Michael returned, she had fixed her hair, applied a touch of makeup, and exchanged her robe for gray slacks and a blue vintage tunic.

Handsome sat still for several photos before he stretched leisurely, padded to the window, and looked at Eliza meaningfully.

She opened the window for him. "You be careful out there. I'll expect you back in the morning." When Eliza turned she saw Michael's amused expression. "What?"

"You sounded like the mother of a teenager."

"If I were, I'd say, 'be home by eleven'. That's what Hendrika used to say when I stayed with her."

"My mom used to add, 'Don't drink and drive'."

"Good advice. Speaking of driving, we better go."

"Are you coming with me?" Michael asked.

Eliza looked at her watch. Regretfully she shook her head. "I'd love to, but I'd better go straight to work from the hospital."

When Eliza pulled into the supermarket complex, Michael followed her. He parked next to her and waited while she dashed inside.

Idly he noticed a green pickup passing their cars. A few seconds passed before the significance of this registered. Eliza had said she thought just such a vehicle had been following her. He jumped out of his truck, but by then the pickup was too far away for him to get the license plate number.

He muttered a few forceful words for being so slow to react. Still, his MP training had kicked in enough to notice the make and model of the truck and the fact that it had an Illinois plate. But he knew that was not enough to find it. There had to be hundreds of green pickups in and around Chicago. Besides, Eliza had not been absolutely certain that she had been followed. Still the mere thought of some deviant creep stalking her enraged and terrified him.

When Eliza came back to her car, she was carrying something wrapped in the green tissue paper florists used. A bouquet of flowers or a potted plant? He waved at her with a smile, thinking how characteristic of her it was to be thoughtful enough to take flowers to Winona. This small act of kindness endeared her to him even more. As if he needed more reasons to . . . like her. Reluctantly, Michael acknowledged that he did a lot more than like her, but he was not ready to give those powerful feelings a name.

All the way to the hospital he looked for the green pickup but there was no sign of it. Instead, a white van stayed in the left lane next to Eliza. Michael maneuvered his truck into a position from which he could clearly see the license plate and wrote the number on the back of his sketch book.

The van followed them into the parking lot. It quickly passed their parked cars and took off. Though Michael was tempted to follow it, he decided against it. Judging by the stream of people leaving the hospital, they had only a few minutes before visiting hours were over.

On the maternity floor they spotted John standing in front of the nursery window. He wore a hospital gown over his clothes and greeted them with a huge grin.

"That's her," he said, pointing to the last bassinet, his

voice a mix of awe and pride. "All seven pounds and five ounces of her."

Eliza pressed her face against the window. "Look at all that black hair," she exclaimed. "She's absolutely darling."

Michael clapped his hand on John's shoulder. "You did good, partner."

Eliza rolled her eyes. "Seems to me Winona had a little something to do with this."

John grinned, "Yeah, let's go see her."

They picked up gowns at the nurses' station and put them on.

"Winona, your daughter is adorable," Eliza said. "Have you picked out a name yet?"

"Dena. And Eliza for her middle name, if you don't mind."

Eliza blushed with pleasure. "I'm honored."

"Thanks to you, we got the loan," John added.

"You got it because your business proposition was sound. I merely gave you a few hints." That was true. Peter had not needed a collateral guarantee from her.

"Thanks anyway," Michael added. "I'm sure it was your advice that got us the loan." He smiled at her warmly.

"I was glad to help." Turning to Winona and removing the tissue paper from the flowers, Eliza said, "I brought you these."

"How lovely," Winona said, admiring the pink sweetheart roses and white baby's breath arranged in a porcelain tea pot. "Thank you."

"You're welcome. My grandmother is making a

baby quilt for you. She started it the day after she met you at my place, and knowing her, it's probably just about finished."

"How nice of her to do that when she barely knows us."

"She loves doing needle work and when she has someone specific to make something for, she's doubly glad."

The nurse entered, carrying the baby. "Visiting hours are over," she announced as she handed the baby to Winona.

"Could we just see the baby before we leave?" Eliza asked.

"Do it quickly," she said, her tone brisk.

"Do you want to hold her?" Winona asked.

"Me?" Eliza wanted to do just that but was a bit apprehensive. "I don't have much experience with babies—actually, none."

"Use one hand to support her head and then hold her like this." Winona demonstrated and smiled encouragingly at Eliza.

"How do you know this?" Eliza asked, taking the baby gingerly.

"I was the oldest one in a family of five kids. I had lots of practice."

Eliza looked at the baby. "Hi, there, Dena Eliza. Aren't you the prettiest little girl," she crooned.

Michael watched Eliza and something inside him lurched sideways. His heart, perhaps? She looked so natural holding the baby. How did women do that? Without practice or previous experience they could hold a baby securely, happily, and even bond with it spontaneously, he suspected. Could men do that?

Studying John, who looked a little loopy but had a huge grin on his face, Michael wondered if he would react the same way if he became a father. He had no clue. He watched Eliza again and felt a surge of emotion hit him hard enough to make breathing difficult. Maybe with Eliza—

"Hey, partner. I see you brought your camera. How about snapping a few shots to send to the folks?" John asked.

"Yeah, sure." Michael was glad that John had torn him from the dangerous thoughts that had sneaked into his brain. He took a couple of pictures of Eliza with the baby before she could protest and hand Dena Eliza to her mother. Michael continued to take shots of the new family until the nurse returned. She looked pointedly at her watch.

"It's ten minutes past visiting hours," she said. "You two must leave now. And *you*," she nodded toward John, "can stay five more minutes. That's all."

Meekly Eliza and Michael said their good-byes and left.

In the parking lot, Michael took Eliza's arm to stop her. "Where are you going? Your truck is parked over there."

Eliza blinked. "You're right." They walked a few paces before she spoke again. "Isn't she just precious? Did you see how small her hands are, and her fingers? But so perfect at the same time."

Her voice was filled with wonder. And could it be longing? "Yeah, I saw."

They reached her truck. Eliza unlocked the door but did not get in immediately. "I'm glad you came to the apartment to tell me about Winona's baby. I wouldn't have missed this for the world. Thanks."

"You're welcome." She was wearing her hair loose. Michael could not keep his hands from touching it. As a painter he was preoccupied with color and texture. And the rich color and texture of Eliza's hair was again pleasing to his touch. His fingers moved to her face. Her skin, smooth and warm with the radiant glow of health, fueled his longing to keep touching her. Even as the cautious voice in his conscience urged him to back off, reminding him to concentrate on his art, he lowered his head to kiss her.

For now he wanted to focus on this woman who had crept into his life. Crept? Hardly. He had invited her, welcomed her, never suspecting that she would become so important to him. How she had become such a vital part of his world did not matter. What mattered was that he felt her arms embracing him, her fingers gently stroking his back, her lips returning his kisses, her fragrance filling his senses.

When Eliza firmly pushed him away, Michael did not know how much time had passed or how many kisses they had exchanged. Shakily he asked, "What?"

Eliza took several tremulous breaths before she spoke. "Two things. One, I promised always to stop you; and two, I have to go to work."

"Oh."

"Yeah, oh." She smiled at him. "Go home, Michael. I'll see you in the morning, right?"

Morning? She must have noticed his perplexed expression because Eliza felt it necessary to remind him that he was painting her. He watched her drive off with a wave of her hand.

Chapter Nine

Still under the spell of those kisses, Michael stood still, staring after Eliza's truck. He did not notice the two men until it was too late. He deflected the first punch at his face with his right shoulder, but the force of it was strong enough to send him backwards into the second man who gripped him in a bear hug from behind. He was a big man.

"Stay away from the girl," the assailant said.

"What?" He could not ask anything else as the first man rushed toward him again. Michael drew his knees to his chest and straightening his legs, kicked the attacker in the rib cage. The man stumbled back and went down.

With an unearthly yell John rushed toward them and joined the melee. For the next minute or so grunts filled the air, fists connected with body parts and then suddenly the fight was over as Michael's attackers fled into the darkness.

143

John was bent over, his hands resting on his knees, panting. When he could, he said, "Cuz, good thing I showed up when I did. What was that about?"

"Darned if I know." Michael leaned against his truck. He wiped the blood off his mouth. "They jumped me."

"Did they try to rob you?"

Michael shook his head. "More like warn me off."

"About what?"

"The exact words were, 'Stay away from the girl'."

"What girl? Eliza?" John's voice held a disbelieving note.

"She's the only girl in my life right now."

John frowned. "It makes no sense to warn you to stay away from Eliza. Or is there something I don't know? Like a jealous boyfriend?"

Michael shook his head. "Eliza never mentioned a boyfriend and we've known each other now for what? A little over three months?" He looked at his left hand. The knuckles were skinned. "She did mention a Rick, but I had the impression that he wasn't important to her."

"Maybe *she's* important to *him*," John suggested.

Michael did not like that idea. He rotated his left shoulder which hurt. "It's been a long time since we've been in a fight."

"Yeah. Not since we broke up the brawl in that San Diego bar. What was it called? Salvation? Last Resort? Something like that. Remember?"

Michael's attempted grin turned into a grimace. "That was some fight. We both needed first aid."

"Like now. Good thing we're at a hospital. Let's get some ice packs."

When Michael opened the door for Eliza the next morning, she gasped.

"What happened to your face?"

Michael felt a little embarrassed for having been caught with his guard down. He shrugged, "Two guys jumped me. My fault for not paying attention. I still had my mind on a certain distracting woman and her sweet kisses."

"Hey, I'm not the one who started the kissing," Eliza reminded him. "Of course, I didn't object." When she saw his raised eyebrow, she added, "Oh, all right, so I rather enjoyed it. And I'm not sorry either," she said, her chin lifted.

She looked at him, challenging him to blame her for enjoying the kisses. When he did not, Eliza added, "I'm sorry, though, that you got hurt. Your poor mouth." She rose on tiptoe and brushed a whisper of a kiss on his bruised lips.

"Kiss and make it feel better?" Michael asked, his voice husky.

"Something like that."

When she looked as if she might kiss him again, he said, "Eliza, don't start anything you're not prepared to follow through on."

"Who said I'm not prepared to finish what I start?" Realizing that perhaps she was not quite as prepared as she claimed, she added, "Even though I'm not backing down, we do have to work. But before we start, tell me exactly what happened."

Michael did.

Eliza looked at him thoughtfully. "So, this wasn't a mugging. Did they say anything?"

Michael looked toward the easel, hoping his expression did not betray him, hoping she would drop the matter.

"They did say something."

"What?"

So much for glossing over the incident. Maybe they ought to discuss it. He told her what the men had said. Eliza looked stricken.

"Who's this girl they warned you about? You never mentioned you had a girl."

Michael's mouth opened in surprise. Then he shook his head. "Since you're the only girl in my life, I assumed it was you," Michael said and walked to his easel.

Eliza felt such joy that she wanted to grab Michael and dance him around the studio and kiss him senseless.

"Which brings us to the men who jumped me in the parking lot. Who's your boyfriend or ex-boyfriend who's so passionate about you that he'd hire two thugs to discourage me?"

Eliza's eyes grew saucer-like. She blurted out the first thing that came into her mind. "Did he succeed in discouraging you?"

"No way!"

Eliza tried to suppress the pleased smile that teased the corner of her mouth.

"Who is he?" Michael asked.

She shook her head, perplexed. "That's just it. Nobody was ever that passionate about me." She paused for a second. "Unless it's Rick, but he—"

"You've mentioned Rick before. Who is he?"

Eliza gestured dismissingly, "Rick's somebody I've dated on and off for the past three or four years, but he's not passionate about me. Trust me on that. He's sort of a friend of the family. He and my mother get along better than he and I ever did. She *approves* of him."

Michael felt a stab of jealousy. Eliza's mother would never approve of him in the same way. "Let me guess . . . he's Caucasian, upper-middle class, college-educated, has a nine-to-five junior executive job—"

"So? You're college-educated, too. You have a talent others would kill for, you don't squander your talent but work hard at it . . ." Seeing Michael's expression, she stopped. "What?"

"I like the way you defend me."

Eliza felt warmth flame her cheeks. She suddenly realized how easily she had rushed to his defense. No way would she allow Michael to feel inferior to Rick. As far as she was concerned, there was no comparison, not even in appearance. Rick had those college fraternity boy looks that appealed to many women, but Michael's sharply chiseled features and his blue-black hair gave him an edgy, masculine aura she found irresistible.

"Is there any reason this Rick would hire someone to beat me up?"

The question caught her by surprise. Fortunately,

Michael was concentrating on mixing colors on his palette and was not looking at her. She had a moment to prepare an answer.

"I can't think of a logical reason why Rick or anyone I know would do that," she said even as an ugly suspicion wormed its way into her mind. She would have to think about it when she was alone and could concentrate.

"What did the two men look like?" she asked.

"One was big, as big as John, but older. The other was smaller but scrappy. The kind of guy who fights dirty, who'd kick a man when he's down. I'd say they were professionals who hire out their services. Their bad luck was that they tangled with two ex-military cops."

"Did you report the incident to the police?" she asked.

"The hospital insisted on it when John and I went inside for a little first aid."

Eliza rushed to his side. "You didn't hurt your right hand, did you?"

In reply Michael lifted his hand for her to see.

She touched his hand gently. "Thank heaven," Eliza murmured, the enormous relief she felt audible in her voice. "You must be super careful. If you'd injured your painting hand and couldn't have your show . . . ," she could not finish the dreadful thought. "Promise you'll be careful."

Except for his mother, Michael could not remember anyone having been particularly concerned over his well-being. Deeply touched, he said, "I promise. Now go and get changed so we can get started."

While she changed into the slip, Eliza could not think about anything except the attack on Michael. Was Rick capable of instigating such an attack? Did he even know the kind of people who could be hired to beat up someone? Eliza had trouble envisioning Rick in the company of such men—unless his motivation was exceedingly strong.

But what would motivate Rick to be involved in such a reprehensible act? Eliza had no answer. Maybe the motivation came from Rick's business problems. It seemed so unlikely that Eliza shook her head. After all, he had resources and connections. Still, she would pursue the possibility. She would give her stepfather another call. One thing was certain: If Rick was responsible for Michael being attacked, he would pay for it. Eliza would see to it if it was the last thing she ever did.

Eliza pushed the sleeve of her blouse up to glance at her watch. Her stepfather was taking a long lunch break. Suppressing a yawn, she decided to wait another fifteen minutes. Any longer than that and her sleep would be seriously shortchanged.

She had posed an extra hour, not wanting to interrupt Michael who had been painting with concentration that had been inspiring to watch. He worked silently, with only an occasional low remark to himself, such as "tone down the red," or "add a little ochre to the green."

His focus on the painting had allowed her to steal looks at him to her heart's content. And how she loved those stolen glances. Occasionally she forced herself to look straight ahead for long minutes, fearing that he would become aware of the intensity of her feelings and that it might disrupt the creative process.

That morning the radio station had played Beethoven's Ninth which Eliza had never heard in its entirety. The last movement with the chorus raising its voice to a glorious crescendo had pulled Michael back to reality. He had apologized for keeping her so long and rewarded her with a spontaneous kiss. And what a kiss it had been. For such a kiss she would—

"Hello, Eliza. I hope I haven't kept you waiting too long. The men I took to lunch were in no hurry."

Eliza caught a whiff of her stepfather's breath and knew it had been a three-martini meal. That surprised her. He rarely indulged during the day. Was the uncertain stock market giving him trouble? Even experienced traders like Charles could sustain heavy losses in a wildly unpredictable and fluctuating market.

Charles asked his secretary to bring them coffee.

Once they were seated in his office and the secretary had brought in two cups of strong coffee, Eliza wasted no time. "I need to find out if Rick's company is in trouble. I wouldn't ask, but this is important."

Charles paused, thinking, then he shrugged. "This isn't a secret." He sweetened his coffee and sipped some before he continued. "The news isn't good. I haven't said anything to your mother yet, so I'd appreciate it if you didn't either."

"I won't. This conversation is strictly between us," Eliza assured him.

"Carr Industries has a serious cash flow problem. Several million dollars in ready money would bail them out. Your trust fund would be just about the right size to do that."

"When pigs fly!" Eliza exclaimed.

"Good girl. Don't get snookered into anything."

"Has Rick tried getting a loan?"

"He's trying, but loans have to be paid back. A wife doesn't."

"I'll have to introduce Rick to some of my friends from school. There wasn't a poor girl among them. And most of them had trust funds considerably bigger than mine."

"And then your father owns a bank. He might not make a loan to a mere acquaintance, but to a son-in-law . . . ? That's a different ball game. You're a great catch, Eliza."

Eliza grimaced in distaste. "Thanks for telling me all this, Charles. I won't take up any more of your time."

"No problem, dear girl. You've got a good head on your shoulders, Eliza. Don't let any man tell you differently."

"I won't. You can count on that."

Charles walked her to the door.

Eliza drove home. Deep in thought, she did not notice the green pickup until she reached her apartment complex. A shiver of fear raced through her. It was quickly replaced by anger.

"Great, I led them right to my front door," she muttered, disgusted with herself. She glanced up and down the street. There were a number of people walking past and cars pulling in and out of the parking lot. She waved to some of her neighbors. She did not think she was in any danger.

With fast, determined steps she approached the pick-up from the rear. The two men apparently did not see her until she jerked open the door on the driver's side.

"Gentlemen, I strongly advise you to stop following me. Whatever Rick is paying you isn't enough to risk tangling with the guys my father will sic on you. And he isn't paying you enough to risk tangling with me either. I can throw a fit the likes of which you've never seen. I can scream so loud that nobody will have to phone the cops. They'll hear me from here."

The men stared at her open-mouthed.

"Do I make myself clear?"

Both men nodded.

"Tell Rick to stop playing games. Now get out of here." Eliza slammed the door shut.

They took off, burning rubber.

Now she would have to confront Rick face-to-face. She had to find out if he hired the men to follow her and to attack Michael. She did not expect Rick to confess, but that distinctive jerking of his left shoulder would tell her if he was lying. If she could be reasonably sure Rick was not involved, or if he was, and she could not persuade him to desist, she would call the police. Enough was enough.

* * *

"What do you mean, the woman talked to you? What woman?" Rick asked, his voice irritated.

"The woman you hired us to follow," Jocko said.

"She talked to you?"

"Walked right up to the truck, opened the door before we knowed what was happening and told us to stop following her. And said to tell you to stop playing games. That is, if you're Rick." Jocko was pleased to see Rick's reaction, which was far from pleased.

Rick fiddled with the knot in his tie to give him time to master his irritation. Eliza was feisty. No doubt about that. It was a pity she was not more like her mother. He had his work cut out for him, transforming her into the perfect CEO's wife. But he could do it if he could get her away from that painter. Best to get on with it.

Focusing on the two men he had hired, he said, "I have a new plan. Listen to me carefully. Here's what I want you to do."

When he finished, Jocko and Big Bob exchanged a look.

"What?" Rick demanded.

"We've never done nothin' like that," Jocko said.

"Cuttin' up paintings don't seem right," Big Bob added.

"What? You're suddenly an art lover?" Rick asked with a sneer.

"I like pictures," Big Bob said.

This was coming from a guy who pronounced the word "pitchers." Rick once again regretted ever hiring these two dimwits.

"Listen and listen good," he said. "By now you're so deep into this deal, you can't back out. And don't even think of going to the cops. They'll lock you up and throw away the key. I'm not asking you to cut up a person—just some paintings. What's the big deal?"

Jocko had less trouble with the idea of knifing a man than with slashing paintings. He could not explain why he felt that way, only that he did.

"Do this and do it right and you won't have to do anything else connected with the painter or the woman," Rick promised. "And I'll pay double your usual fee."

"Double?" Big Bob asked.

"Yes."

"And this will be the last time?"

"Yes, Jocko, the last time."

The next day Michael put the finishing touches on Eliza's portrait. Then they walked to a nearby Mexican restaurant. Over plates of tacos they discussed the possible subjects he could paint next for his exhibition.

"You could do anything and it'd be excellent," Eliza said, completely convinced of that.

Michael reached across the table to hold her hand. "Your faith in my ability is wonderful. Don't think that I don't appreciate it. I do, more than you can imagine."

"My faith in you is not misplaced. Don't you know how good you are?"

He shrugged, "but it's nice to hear it confirmed by someone else. Especially if the someone is you."

"Why especially me?" she asked, loving the feel of her hand in his.

"You know why." He raised her hand to his mouth and kissed it. "Because of this. How good it feels to touch each other. How much we like being together, even if we don't talk, if all we do is paint and pose. And you know art."

Eliza breathed shallowly, afraid she might break the tender mood and the unaccustomed stream of words. Michael did not talk much, and did not feel the need to fill any silence with idle chatter the way Rick did. Why was she even thinking of Rick? Probably because she had not been able to reach him to warn him to stay away from Michael—and to keep his goons away from him as well.

She had learned from her mother that Rick was in town. Ordinarily a phone call from her brought an immediate response from him. But this time he was obviously avoiding her. Was he up to something again? Had he ignored the warning she had sent via the thugs who had been following her? Rick was arrogant and opinionated. He did not take advice or suggestions willingly.

"I was thinking," Michael said, stroking Eliza's hand. "I haven't done any urban scenes."

"I love them," Eliza exclaimed. "Remember all those Edward Hopper paintings full of urban loneliness and alienation? Not that you should imitate him. I only mention him because I think he's good. You do *your* take on life in a big city."

"I will. That means I'll have to prowl the streets with my camera to find subjects."

"You sound like you look forward to doing that."

"I do. I'll start this afternoon."

"In that case, let's go."

They walked back to the studio. When they approached the front door Michael stopped, holding Eliza back.

"What on earth? Looks like the lock's been jimmied. Stay back," he whispered as he pushed the door open quietly.

Eliza had no intention of staying back. She followed him. As soon as they entered, they heard noises from the studio.

"It don't seem right to cut up this pretty picture," Big Bob said. "Looks just like her, don't it?"

"Yeah. And over here are a whole bunch more. The guy sure works hard."

Eliza touched Michael's arm. He laid his finger across his lips and then sprinted around the partition. With a fierce yell he lunged at the big guy.

The men were so astonished, they froze for a moment, giving Eliza a chance to grab her pepper spray from her purse. She aimed it at the small guy. "Stay there," she warned, but when he stepped forward and pushed her so that she fell against the edge of the small table, she aimed the can upward and pushed the spray button. He backed off with a howl. Unfortunately she was too close to him or her aim was off and some of the spray got her as well.

Then John walked in. "What the . . ." Assessing the

situation quickly and seeing that Michael had the big guy in a hammer lock, he grabbed the smaller guy and twisted his arm behind him. "I thought we dealt with you guys in the parking lot. Some people are slow learners."

Eliza dialed 911.

It took almost an hour for the police officers to take statements. The intruders admitted that they had been hired but maintained that they did not know the man's name or anything about him. They did know the make and model of his car but had not written down the license plate number. They thought they could identify him in a police lineup.

Michael and John nailed boards over the front door until the lock could be fixed. They would use the back door in the meantime. John went home after helping secure the place.

Eliza had a slight bump on her head and a headache but refused to go to the hospital.

"Then I'm taking you to your grandmother's. You shouldn't be alone in case you have a concussion. Are you sure you don't want me to take you to the hospital?" Michael asked again.

"I'm positive. All they'd do is give me an aspirin." She gave Michael directions to Hendrika's place and used her cell phone to call her grandmother to let her know they were on their way.

Michael drove past the gate twice, double-checking the numbers that were discreetly hewn into the two stone pillars flanking the high brick walls. This was not a house. This was a mansion. He glanced at Eliza who sat next to him, her eyes closed. Could she have made a mistake and given him the wrong address?

Michael looked up and down the street. The entire neighborhood reeked of money, social status, and prestige. Could Eliza's family really live here? Had she pretended all this time to be poor because she was playing him for a fool? Toying with him? Part of him did not want to believe this. Eliza was not like that. And yet here he was, parked in front of this mansion.

She had lied to him. There was no escaping that fact. She had lied not by what she told him, but by what she had not. Was a lie of omission more venial? Maybe. He did not really know, but the lack of trust it implied hurt every bit as much as an outright lie. He felt as if his heart had been torn out of his living chest.

"Eliza, wake up." Michael shook her shoulder gently. "I know you're tired and your head hurts, but you have to wake up."

She opened her eyes. Seeing him, she smiled sleepily, sweetly—a smile that was open, warm, and trusting. How could she smile and look at him like that when she knew she had deceived him? Confused and hurt, he looked away.

"Where are we?" she asked.

"You tell me. We're facing an electronic gate and a long, winding drive behind it."

Eliza rolled down her window and addressed the camera mounted on the gate. "This is Eliza Marshall and Michael Yuma, here to see my grandmother."

Moments later the gate swung open.

Michael did not say anything until he parked the car.

He stared at the three-story house for several seconds. Finally he asked, his voice tight. "Your grandmother lives here?"

"Yes."

The front door was flung open and Sturges rushed toward them.

"Are you all right, Miss Eliza?" Sturges asked.

"I'm fine. You've met Michael, haven't you?"

"Yes. How are you, Mr. Yuma? Please come on in. Mrs. Marshall is waiting for you in the sitting room."

Chapter Ten

Hendrika was waiting for them in the sitting room. Eliza hugged her grandmother.

"Come, let's sit down while Sturges fetches the pitcher of lemonade he made. You two must be thirsty on such a hot day," Hendrika said. Only then did she look closely at her granddaughter. "Eliza, what's wrong with your eyes? They look swollen."

"I got some pepper spray in them. It's not too bad." Then she had to tell the whole story.

Hendrika shook her head. "And these two men are the same ones who've been following you? The ones you used to send a warning to Rick?"

Eliza nodded. She leaned back against the couch and closed her eyes. It felt good to have them closed. Her eyes burned more than she had let on.

"And they were really going to destroy your paintings when you walked in on them?"

160

"It looked that way."

"How awful. I hope the police can prove who hired them and get the guilty individual. Imagine destroying works of art! Eliza," Hendrika paused. "My poor darling's eyes keep drifting shut. I think she's losing her battle with sleep. After what she's been through I'm not surprised."

"If you tell me what room she'll sleep in, I'll carry her there," Michael offered.

"That's kind of you. Her old room is upstairs, the third door on the right."

Michael carried Eliza upstairs. He paused in the doorway to make a quick survey of the room. He did not know much about antique furniture but he did recognize good lines and first-rate workmanship when he saw it.

The room was large, well-proportioned, and beautiful. Michael tried to reconcile this bedroom with the small one in Eliza's apartment. He could not. They were worlds apart.

Gently he laid Eliza on a bed that had an elaborately-carved headboard. He removed her shoes before he covered her with the crocheted afghan that had been folded at the foot of the bed. He allowed himself to study her for a moment.

She was the same woman he had known and painted and fallen for during the past three months—and yet she was not. Something very subtle seemed different about her. Or was this minute difference due to the fact that now he knew so much more about her? Did that mean the difference was in him and that Eliza was the same? He did not know. He turned to go.

"Don't go yet," Eliza murmured. "Stay a bit. Sit beside me."

Looking at her eyes, he felt guilty. He had failed to protect her. It was his fault her eyes were swollen and must burn like the devil. He sat on the bed and took her hand.

"You've got to move your paintings. They're not safe in your studio. Michael, you have to!"

"I will. Don't worry. I'll take care of them."

"Maybe the Kuenstler Gallery can take them. If not, you can stash them in my apartment. I doubt that anyone will think to look for them there. Besides, I have an alarm system." Eliza told him the code. "I know you're upset with me because of all this," she said, gesturing around the elegant room, "but I really want to help you get your paintings shown. You have to believe that."

"I do."

"You do?"

"And I appreciate the offer of help. I really do. Thanks, Eliza. Now go to sleep. It is way past your bedtime and you've been through quite an ordeal." Michael bent down and kissed her softly on her forehead.

Downstairs in the sitting room, a small painting caught his eye.

When Hendrika came to stand beside him, he said, "It's an original. I've never known anyone who owned an original van Gogh."

"My grandfather bought this painting shortly after van Gogh's death, for a very small sum. Poor Vincent's greatness wasn't recognized during his lifetime. But you know that. You don't need an art history lesson from me. Come and have something to eat."

Hendrika linked her arm through his and led him to the kitchen.

"Where's Miss Eliza?" Sturges asked.

"She fell asleep on the couch. Michael carried her upstairs. Let's sit down." Hendrika motioned Michael to a chair.

Looking at the pitcher of lemonade and individual bowls of fruit salad, his mouth watered in anticipation.

Hendrika, ever considerate, let him drink and eat before she brought up the subject uppermost in her mind.

"Since the man behind this scheme—Rick—isn't in custody yet, you're not out of danger. Or rather your paintings aren't. I have a suggestion. Why don't you bring them here. Sturges could drive one truck and you the other. This house is as safe as you can make a private residence. Wouldn't it make sense to do that?"

"I've worried about their safety," Michael admitted. "The gallery doesn't have enough space to store them."

"What about *your* safety?" Hendrika asked.

"I think I can handle this Rick character."

"He might hire more men to come after you."

"My friend John will help me. I might crash at his place for the night. He and I were a good team when we used to break up fights." When Hendrika looked puzzled, he added, "John and I were military cops." Michael rose. "Thanks for the offer, but I'll be okay.

But I would like to store my paintings here. I'll get John to help me bring them. Now I'd better go. I have a lot to do."

"I'll walk you to the door," Hendrika said. On the way she said, "I'll be eternally grateful to you for helping Eliza. My granddaughter means more to me than I can say."

"You don't need to thank me, Mrs. Marshall. How could I not have helped her? Besides, she got into all this because she spent time with me."

"You like her, don't you?"

"Yes."

"More than like? You must. You were ready to risk your life for her."

"Yes," Michael admitted, his tone clipped.

"But?" Hendrika probed.

"But Eliza lied to me. She deceived me."

Hendrika sighed, "I know. I asked her to take a chance and tell you the truth, but she so wanted you to like her for herself."

"She didn't trust me."

"And that hurts," Hendrika said, her voice sympathetic.

"How could she think I'd be after her money?"

"Because a lot of people are, even to the point of attempting to kidnap her when she was just a child."

Michael opened his mouth and then shut it. There was truth to what Hendrika said, of course.

"Please try to understand. Eliza wanted you to see her without being blinded by all this." Hendrika waved her hand at her surroundings. "People are impressed by wealth. Or what it can buy. Michael, even you were by the van Gogh painting."

Taken aback, Michael could not think of anything to say. He nodded a wordless good-bye and left.

Eliza slept until the following afternoon. She felt groggy and disoriented. After a third cup of coffee she finally felt alert enough to ask questions.

"Gran, did anyone call the shelter and tell them why I didn't show up for work yesterday?"

"I did, and I told them you were ill and wouldn't be in today or tomorrow."

"Thanks." Eliza ran her finger around the rim of her coffee cup, wanting to ask about Michael but afraid of the answer to her question.

"He was upset and hurt," Hendrika volunteered, sensing Eliza's anxiety.

"*Very* upset?"

"Yes. He feels you didn't trust him and that hurts."

Eliza bit her lip to keep from crying. "I know you warned me that this might happen."

"But that doesn't make it any easier, does it?"

"No, Gran. Do you think I can make Michael understand why I didn't tell him the truth?"

"I don't know, dear, but if you love him, you'll have to make him understand. You have no choice but to try. It may take some time before Michael comes to terms with this."

Eliza nodded. "I'd better go over there now and get it over with."

"You can't leave the house, Eliza. Not until the doctor has had another look at you. He came yesterday and examined you. Do you remember?"

"Vaguely. He must have given me something to make me sleep this long."

"He did."

"I'm all right. I don't need to see him again."

"Maybe not, but you hit your head and got pepper spray into your eyes. I just want to make sure."

Eliza knew there was no point in arguing with her grandmother, so she spent the next two hours flipping through magazines.

The doctor came and pronounced her fit to leave the house. But before she could, Peter arrived with some news. The police had arrested Rick. His two cohorts had picked him out of a police lineup and identified him as their boss.

"What'll happen to him?" Eliza asked.

Peter shrugged. "That'll depend on how good a lawyer he hires. But no matter what happens in the courts, he's finished in this town. You won't have to worry about him anymore."

"Mom will be so upset. She really liked him and had great plans for him," Eliza said. "I should go and see her."

Gloria's eyes were swollen and red-rimmed. Eliza had never seen her mother look so upset.

"I am so sorry," she said, "I didn't realize Rick was that desperate. To hire gangsters to go after you! To try to destroy paintings!" Gloria collapsed into a chair and sobbed. "How could I have been so wrong about him?"

Her mother was always dramatic but Eliza sensed that this time it was not histrionics. She really was upset by what she had set in motion.

"And there's another thing I did badly. I disapproved of Michael. I'm sorry. He obviously is a different sort of painter. Tell him I'm sorry."

"I don't understand. What sort of painter did you think he was?"

"The kind who says he loves you while you pose for him, but cheats on you the moment the portrait is finished."

"Did you know such a painter?" Eliza asked.

"Yes, I did, when I was eighteen," Gloria paused, trying to stop her tears. "I loved him so. We eloped because my parents didn't want me to marry him, but I did anyway. I was so happy—for a few months. Then he broke my heart, the faithless rat. And then I discovered I was pregnant, and miscarried. It was a very bad experience for me and it took me a long time to get over it. That's why I was trying to keep you away from Michael. I didn't want you to be hurt."

"I'm so sorry, Mom. Why didn't you tell me about your painter?"

"I hated to admit yet another failed relationship."

Eliza was silent. She did not know what to say. She had always assumed that after the pain of the initial breakup of a marriage, her mother quickly forgot and moved on. How wrong she had been. Right then Eliza resolved to get to know this woman better—this woman who was her mother, who had suffered, and had far greater depth of character than she had suspected.

"Why do I always pick the wrong men? Except for your father. He was the only truly decent one of the lot, and I was too immature to recognize that. Why don't I ever learn?"

"But you have learned. Charles is a good man. This time you chose wisely."

Gloria paused. "I did, didn't I? Charles *is* a good husband." She was as much surprised as pleased by this realization.

"Now, I'm getting a warm cloth to wipe your face. Then I'll fix you a cup of herb tea with a shot of medicinal brandy in it."

Gloria smiled. The smile was a little wobbly, it was true, but it happily replaced the tears and recriminations.

"I do love you, even if I don't say it often," Gloria murmured.

For a moment Eliza's heavy heart felt a little lighter.

The next morning Eliza took a long time getting dressed. She changed outfits twice and finally settled on jeans and a bulky cable pullover. It was the sort of outfit she normally wore to work and then to the studio. Except this was not a normal visit to Michael's studio, and it might be her last. No, she could not allow herself to think that way.

When she found herself standing in front of his door, she could not recall a thing about driving there. She stood still for several minutes, going over in her mind what she would say. Finally she raised her hand, knocked, and waited. What if Michael wasn't home?

Or worse, what if he was home but would not let her in? Before she worked herself into a state of frenzied despair, Michael opened the door.

They stared at each other without saying a word for several seconds. He looked as if he had not slept well either. She longed to cradle his face with her hands and kiss the shadows from his eyes. *Pull yourself together. She could do this!*

"May I come in?" Eliza asked, her voice low.

Michael stepped aside and invited her in with a hand gesture. "If you've come to pose, it isn't necessary."

Eliza stopped as if turned to stone. Did that mean he wasn't going to finish—

"The portrait's finished," he said.

"Good," Eliza sighed in relief. "For a moment I thought maybe you'd abandoned it. Wouldn't use it in your show."

"It's good. Why wouldn't I use it?"

"Because of what I did. Kept part of the truth from you."

"At least you're admitting that it wasn't the right thing to do."

"It was wrong. I took a gamble. I . . ." Eliza's voice trailed off. *How could his beautiful eyes look so hard and unforgiving?*

"What did you gamble? That I'd never find out the truth? If you hadn't gotten hurt in our fight with Rick's goons, would you ever have told me about your family, your wealth? The fact that you were a . . . what's the word? Heiress?"

"Of course, I would have told you. I gambled on your not finding out until it didn't matter. Until you liked me for myself."

"What else would I have liked you for? Your money? Do you think I'm that shallow? You've seen my paintings. How could you think so little of me? Or, for that matter, of yourself?"

His dark eyes blazed with indignation. Eliza's hopes collapsed. Michael seemed so hurt and so angry that he could not forgive her—at least not now. But what if he never could? Eliza's throat burned with the tears she tried to hold back. She loved Michael. She had been in love with him for a long time. Maybe right from the beginning.

"Eliza, answer me."

"What do you want me to say? I didn't lie to you deliberately. I told you my name. Everything I told you was the truth. I simply didn't say that my family had money."

"And that was such a small thing to keep secret? So insignificant?"

"Yes! My family's wealth does not define me. I'm more than just money and stock certificates and property."

"True, but to some extent it does define you. Think about it. Wouldn't your life have been different if your father didn't own a bank and heaven knows what else?"

"Yes." Eliza felt defeated. How could she make Michael understand why she had kept the truth from him? She had to try to make him understand.

"Michael, I didn't tell you because when people find

out about my family's wealth they treat me differently. Hear me out, please," she said to forestall his response.

"When I met you and realized you had no idea who I was, I felt as if I'd been reborn. I could be a woman who had a job, an apartment, and every day worries, like making my paycheck last to the end of the month, hoping the truck wouldn't break down, things like that. But best of all, that was who *you* would see, too."

"I did. And did you find that amusing? Here's this unsophisticated, dumb Indian who has no idea—"

"Stop! How can you even think that?" she cried out, appalled. "Now it's my turn to ask how can you think so little of yourself? Of me?"

They looked at each other silently.

"Michael, I watched your face when you saw my grandmother's house. If you're honest, you'll admit that you were impressed. Very impressed. People always are . . . even you." He was silent for so long Eliza feared he would not answer.

Michael finally nodded his head in silent admission.

Eliza felt such relief that her legs trembled. She placed her hand on the back of the nearest chair for support. "Where does that leave us?" she asked, hardly daring to breathe while she waited for his reply.

He shook his head wearily, "I don't know."

At least he had not told her he never wanted to see her again. Hope fluttered in her heart. Quickly, before he could say anything, she spoke.

"Your opening is in less than three weeks. I know how much that means to you. Why don't you concentrate on getting ready? We'll talk after the show." She moved toward the door.

"Eliza."

She stopped.

"I'm still angry with you for not trusting me. For not believing that I could look beyond your wealth and see *you*."

"I'm sorry. Truly I am. I didn't mean to hurt you. Please believe that."

Michael nodded.

"And I do trust you. I trust you with my life. That has to count for something."

He nodded again, "I think a three-week cooling-off period is a good idea. It'll give us both a chance to see how we feel."

Eliza knew exactly how she felt, but she nodded anyway. If he needed time, so be it.

"We'll talk after the show."

Chapter Eleven

The next three weeks seemed like three years to Eliza.

Each time the phone rang, her heart skipped a beat in anticipation. But it was never Michael. Twice, when she did not think she could go through one more day without seeing him, she drove past his studio. Neither time did she so much as catch a glimpse of him, but just looking at his studio made her feel a little better. When she could not sleep, she stared at the watercolor he had given her.

When he had painted the geranium, he had liked her. He had kissed her the way a man kisses a woman he desires. How did he feel now? Did he think of her? If so, was it with anger, or with hurt pride? Or did he also remember their laughter, their talks, and their kisses?

At the shelter Eliza started arts and crafts projects with the girls to alleviate the boredom of endless television-watching. She taught paper-folding. Some of the origami animals they produced were quite good and were used to make mobiles that they sold to a neighborhood store.

Eliza bought one of them and took it to Winona for the baby. They hung the mobile over the crib.

"I think she likes it," Winona exclaimed.

"Of course she does. She's a smart little girl. Look at those bright, intelligent eyes," Eliza said.

"You sure know what to say to make a new mom happy."

"I wish I knew what to say to a certain painter."

"Michael?"

As casually as she could, she asked, "Have you seen him? How is he?"

"Silent, grumpy, moody, miserable. In a snit."

"Me, too. At least I'm miserable. Is he painting?"

"Yeah, but I'm not sure I like what he's painting now. I like his earlier stuff better," Winona said.

"How are the new paintings different?"

"They don't make me feel as good when I look at them. They're sort of lonesome." Winona shrugged, "I don't know enough about art to explain it any better."

"I can't wait to see them," Eliza said, her voice full of yearning.

"Then you're coming to the opening?"

"The gallery sent me an invitation. So unless Michael specifically asks me not to go, I will." If he asked her not to come, she would die. Eliza was sure of that. "Will you see Michael before then?"

"He's having Thanksgiving dinner with us. You'll be at your grandmother's?"

"Yes." Eliza gave the mobile one last twirl. "I better get going."

"He'll get over it," Winona said.

"Michael?"

"Who else are we talking about? He has to lick his wounded pride. You know men and their pride."

"Do you think he will get over it? His wounded pride?" Eliza asked, daring to hope.

"If he's as smart as I think he is, yes. And you can't give up on him. Get in his face. Well, not literally, but don't let him forget you. Do stuff to make him think of you."

Eliza nodded, "Good advice."

When the girls at the shelter baked cookies and frosted them with pumpkin-colored icing, Eliza mailed a dozen to Michael. Her note simple said, "Compliments of the girls from the shelter." He would know who sent them.

The day before Thanksgiving Eliza took a loaf of cranberry bread to Winona.

"My grandmother thought you might like it."

"Thanks, Eliza. Want to stop by tomorrow for some fry bread?" Winona asked.

"I can't. I'm working. And I promised Michael to stay away until the opening."

"I'll mention that you brought the bread . . . just a casual reminder," Winona said with a wink. "It's only a week until the show. I'll see you there. You're not chickening out?"

"No, but I am a little scared," Eliza admitted. She

shivered and forced herself to think of something else.

Actually, she was a lot scared. What if he didn't talk to her? What if he ignored her? Or if he talked to her and told her he decided that he could not forgive her? What if he never wanted to see her again? Such thoughts tormented Eliza until she was sick with worry. Her stomach hurt and she could not keep any food down.

Fleetingly, she considered not going to the show. But when the time came, she put on a lacy slip much like the one Michael had bought for her, a little black dress, and high heeled sandals. Thinking she looked too plain, too openly worried, she added a pair of dangling earrings. She hoped they conveyed a hint of a devil-may-care attitude that she was actually far from feeling.

"That's not her coming in, so you don't have to turn around casually and pretend you're not looking," John said.

"Who's not coming in?" Michael hoped he sounded nonchalant.

"You know who—your favorite model. The girl you're crazy about but too proud to go after," John shook his head.

Michael gave his cousin a sideways glance that suggested John should mind his own business.

"I'm calling it as I see it. You don't eat, you don't sleep, you're grumpier than a sore-tailed mountain lion—"

"Okay. Enough. I get it."

John nudged Michael. "Mrs. Marshall is trying to get our attention over there, by Eliza's portraits."

They walked over to Hendrika.

"I had to wait ten minutes for the crowd to thin out enough to see Eliza's portraits. All your paintings are great, but these portraits are breathtaking."

"Thank you," Michael murmured.

"Look, Cuz, they both have a 'sold' sticker on them."

Michael blinked. "You're right." Turning to Hendrika, he asked, "Mrs. Marshall, did you buy the portraits?"

"I bought one of them—the one with the cat. And Eliza's dad bought the other. I hope you're not upset that we grabbed them with unseemly haste. Of course, they'll stay here for the duration of the exhibition."

"I'm not upset. Where will you hang the portrait?"

"Near the van Gogh. Your painting will be in good company. And I'll loan it to the Art Institute when they have their next exhibition of young artists."

"You sound certain that they'll want to show it," Michael said.

"I *am* certain."

Under ordinary circumstances the prospect of showing his painting in the Art Institute would have made him ecstatic. But he was too worried about Eliza to enjoy the moment. What if he had waited too long? Was John right that he should have gone after her? Probably. Blast his pride.

"Is Eliza coming?" he asked, hoping he masked his anxiety.

"She's here—has been for quite a while," Hendrika said.

"Cuz, you must have blinked," John said with a grin.

"There she is, studying your city scenes," Hendrika said.

"Excuse me," Michael moved toward Eliza, forcing himself not to run. He stopped a few feet away to watch her expression.

She was totally focused on the painting. Michael was not sure how to describe her expression. Rapt? Absorbed? Intent? If he were a conceited man, he would be tempted to call it entranced. Whatever the description, he loved the way she looked at his work. If only she would look at *him* like that.

He came closer. "Eliza?"

She waited a second before she looked at him over her shoulder. "Michael," she said in a soft voice, acknowledging him before she turned back to the painting.

Michael felt disappointment sink through him. He had expected her to . . . what? Throw her arms around him and kiss him, breathless? Yes. It was a lovely fantasy. And it was his own fault that such a welcome was only fantasy. He *had* told her he needed time. What a fool he was. It was time to make amends.

"What do you think?" he asked, stepping close enough to inhale the geranium-laced, green scent he loved and had missed and had smelled in his dreams.

"Of what? The show? It's a great success. I'm sure it'll earn you a terrific review in next Sunday's papers. And it's a commercial success as well, judging by the 'sold' stickers."

"Do *you* think the paintings are a success?"

"Yes. You know I love your work."

If only she loved *him*. "What do you think of my city scenes?"

"They surprised me. They remind me a little of Edward Hopper's work. We talked about him, remember? His urban loneliness."

Michael sucked in his breath. Urban loneliness—he had felt it and painted it during the weeks of their separation, the weeks in purgatory. Eliza had seen it immediately. She had cut straight to the core. That she understood his work better than he did left him shaken.

"What made you feel this loneliness?" she asked.

Michael placed his hands on her shoulders. "You did. Your absence did." He felt her reaction before she spoke.

"I'm so sorry. I never meant to make you feel like that. I'd never want to make anyone feel like that. It's unforgivable."

"It was as much my fault as yours. I'm the one who thought I needed time alone."

"Are you saying you didn't?" Eliza asked, a slight tremble in her voice.

"I needed *you,* not time away from you."

"What are you saying?" she whispered.

"Not here . . ." Michael looked around. Spotting the door that led to the back of the building, he grabbed her hand and pulled her toward it.

Eliza was not reluctant to go with him, but her three-inch heels made walking fast quite difficult.

"Where are we going?" she asked.

"I have no idea, and I don't care, just as long as we're not surrounded by people."

Stepping through the door, they found themselves on the loading dock. He took off his sports jacket and draped it around Eliza's shoulders.

"Not exactly the setting I had in mind, but it'll have to do," Michael said.

"For what?" Eliza asked, looking at him, half afraid, half hopeful.

"For this." Michael pulled her against him and kissed her. For a man as hungry for her as he was, he took his time. When he came up for air, his blood running hot and fiercely through his veins, he cradled her face with his hands and looked into her eyes.

"I missed you, missed you terribly. The light, the light painters love, went out of my world. You know what that means to an artist."

Eliza nodded, too close to tears of relief and joy to speak. Still, she had to know exactly where she stood with him. She could not endure another day of uncertainty.

"I missed you, too—terribly. But where does that leave us? Are you still angry with me? Can you forgive me for not telling you everything? I honestly didn't know how to work something like that into a conversation. 'Oh, by the way, I'm rather well off. Actually, my family is filthy rich'!" To her surprise, Michael chuckled.

"Yeah, that would be a little awkward."

"I should have invited you to lunch at my grandmother's house. That would have shown you the truth."

"But you were afraid."

She nodded.

"Hendrika made me realize that you had legitimate

reasons for your fears. When I saw her van Gogh, I was impressed. Very impressed." Michael paused for a moment. "You know, in a way I'm glad you didn't tell me the truth."

"You are? I don't understand."

"Because now you know I fell in love with you when I thought you were a girl living from paycheck to paycheck like the rest of us."

Eliza wasn't sure she had heard him right. "Did you just say you fell in love with me?"

"Yes. Somewhere between deciding what color your eyes were and trying to capture the way the light gilded your hair and skin, I fell in love. And then I suffered through all those endless weeks of trying to keep my hands off of you. I wasn't sure I'd make it."

Eliza smiled at him, "It's probably shameless of me to admit this, but you didn't have to keep your hands off of me. I didn't want you to. I fell in love with you . . . oh, probably a few minutes after we met."

Michael groaned, "*Now* you tell me." He kissed her again and again.

John opened the door and cleared his throat. "I hate to break this up, but people are asking for you, Cuz."

"Tell them I left," Michael said.

"It's a reporter from the *Tribune*."

"Tell them Michael will be right there," Eliza said. Then to Michael she added, "You have to talk to him. He's important."

"So are you."

"But I'll be here all night. And tomorrow and tomorrow and tomorrow—"

"You'd better be! But one more thing before we go back in there." Casually—because this was the most important question he would ever ask Eliza—he said, "Do you think you could spend your life with a man who smells of turpentine—I mean 24/7—as his wife?"

Eliza threw her arms around Michael. "You have no idea how I love the smell of turpentine. The answer is *yes!*"

"Thank you," Michael murmured. He swallowed twice before he could speak. "Let's run away and get married. You said you didn't like big weddings."

Eliza groaned, "Don't tempt me, Michael. But my grandmother would be so disappointed if we eloped. If I promise we'll have a small wedding at Hendrika's house right after Christmas, will you go and talk to the reporter?"

"Three weeks? That seems so long," Michael protested.

"I know. The last three weeks were endless."

"Nothing like that is ever going to happen again. Nothing will tear us apart—*ever* again. Trust me," Michael said.

"I do." And Eliza did, with all her heart.